MY FANGTASTICALLY EVIL VAMPIRE PET

MO O'HARA

ILLUSTRATED BY MAREK JAGUCKI

SQUARE
FISH

FEIWEL AND FRIENDS ❧ NEW YORK

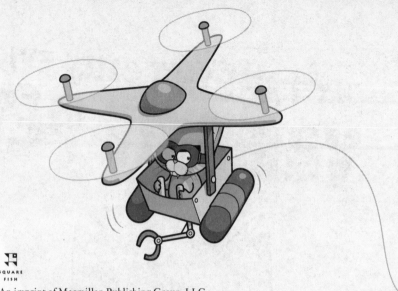

This book is dedicated to all the epic kids
out there who want to make the world
a better place in big ways and small ways.
Storymaking is a great place to start.

MY BIG BAD EVIL SUMMER

This summer is going to be Epic. Epically Evil...or Evilly Epic, or maybe even both.

Whatever. Anyway, this summer is gonna rock 'cause for the first time I'm going away to Evil Scientist Summer camp.

This is going to be the start of something big, so I thought I should write it down. That way when I'm a massively important Evil Scientist in the future and my minions ask, "Oh, Great and Powerful Mark ('cause they'll totally call me that), how did you start out?" I can say, "I can't be bothered to tell you. Read the book."

Mwhaaaa-haaa-haa-haaa-haaa.

1

TOP FIVE REASONS WHY EVIL SCIENTIST SUMMER CAMP IS GOING TO BE AWESOME...

5. It's an Evil Scientist Summer Camp! We learn evil stuff they don't teach (or aren't allowed to teach) at regular school, like traps, disguises and some basic Evil Henchmen 101 stuff. Plus there's evil tennis and swimming and stuff too.

4. There are no annoying little brothers around.

3. There are no annoying zombie goldfish around.

2. My best friend, Sanj (who is an Evil Computer Genius), is going too.

(Well OK, maybe it's a stretch to call Sanj my best friend. One time he trapped me in a booby trap with an actual blue-footed booby [I mean the bird]. He's zapped me with a Supersonic Nicifying Helpful Minion Ray. He's tricked me, cheated me, lied to me and generally betrayed me most of the time, but hey, when you're mostly evil, you don't have a lot of friends to choose from, you know. Maybe I should call him an Evil Colleague. Like if we were both working in an evil job somewhere, he would be in the next evil cubicle. Yeah, that's probably right.)

And 1. I'm smuggling my truly evil pet vampire kitten, Fang, into the camp.

Fang prowled around all my stuff for camp that I had laid out on the bed. She circled and clawed at my Evil Scientist coat and then started swatting at the buttons.

"Fang!" I grabbed it off her, but she clung to the hem of the coat. "Let go. You'll mess it up."

"Meeeeooooooowwww!" she replied as she pulled in her claw and let herself drop inside my bag.

"I gotta put the other stuff in first, Fang." I scooped her out, and she strutted around the bed, scratching at all the rest of my stuff. Which I think in Cat is kinda like her marking all my stuff as her stuff.

"I have to make sure I got everything they said to bring to camp. Then you can get back in."

Fang purred.

"Right . . ."

---

1. White Evil Scientist coat—check
2. Protective laser, hypno- and radiation-proof glasses—check
3. Evil Plans Notebook—check (Sanj and I have already been working on some super-evil plans to show the Evil Scientist Summer camp leaders)
4. Evil disguises, props, traps, secret-code stuff, chemicals, wire, paper clips and tape (it's amazing how many times a decent evil trap needs tape)—check
5. Swim trunks and a towel—check

And I'll just add one. . . .

6. Evil scientist sidekick pet that, according to the rules, you are totally not allowed to bring at all—check!!!

I can't believe the Evil Scientist Summer Camp doesn't allow pets. I mean, yeah, so some people have allergies and stuff, but seriously, we're working with toxic chemicals, explosives and lethal robo-drones (probably—oh, please, let there be lethal robo-drones). But pets are the worst things they can think of?

I'm just saying that if you're gonna start sneezing or breaking out in hives if you get near a little pet fur, then maybe world domination is a little ambitious, don't ya think? Maybe just take over the parts of the world with good air filters.

I looked down at Fang and stroked her behind the ear. "Why would they be so worried about a stupid cat?"

Fang swiped at my hand. "Meeeeeooowwww."

"Owwww! Sorry, Fang," I said, shaking my scratched hand. "I wasn't calling you stupid."

❧   ❧   ❧

"Mark, honey! Time to go!" Mom yelled up
from downstairs. "We're supposed to be at your
Eco-Scientist Camp in two hours, and it's a long
drive!"

Oh, yeah. I didn't mention that, did I? Sanj put
a filter on the website for the camp so it looked
like it's an "Eco-Scientist Camp" for, like, green,
nature-friendly science. Result!

Both my mom and Sanj's mom fell for it. They
filled out the form and paid up straightaway.

"I'm so pleased you're taking an interest in
environmental issues, Mark," Mom had said.

"What issues?" I'd asked before Sanj elbowed
me. "I mean, yeah, of course. I'm totally green,
right."

"You know, this might be a lovely thing for
Tom and Pradeep to do as well," Sanj's mom
had suggested. "Wouldn't it be nice to have an
adventure with your younger brothers?"

"Noooooo!" Sanj and I had yelled at the same
time.

"They would totally wreck it," I'd said. Fang jumped on my shoulder and meowed her agreement.

Sanj took a deep breath. "Tom and Pradeep might lack the maturity to participate fully in the intense discussions and activities of the camp," he'd said with his evilest smile.

It had taken me a second to figure out what Sanj had said, but once I did, I said, "Yeah, that."

"I suppose you're right. You are older," Mrs. Kumar had said. "It will be lovely for you boys to discuss the impact of global warming on the environment, and maybe your young minds will find a solution."

"And get cold polar bears ice hats too," Sami, Sanj's little sister, had said, tugging on the sleeve of my white coat.

"Polar bear ice hats?" I'd asked.

"TV said polar bear ice hats are too

small." Sami frowned. "They need bigger hats."

Sanj had leaned over. "It's the polar *ice caps* that are shrinking, Sami. Not ice hats that the bears wear . . . ," he'd trailed off. "Never mind. Yes, yes, we'll get hats for the bears."

And that was it. We were signed up for Evil Scientist Summer Camp faster than you could say "Evil Scientist Water Polo, anyone?!"

2

Mom's car pulled up at the gate to the campsite. The sign out front read:

WELCOME TO
CAMP MWHAAA-HAA-HA-A-WATHA

It looked just like it did on the website. We were actually here! I could feel a major "Mwhaaa-haa-haa-haa" inside me bursting to get out.

Sanj's mom leaped out of the passenger seat of the car and opened the trunk. "It's so exciting for you boys." She beamed.

My mom unclipped Sami's car seat, and Sami bounced out and opened the door.

"Wanna go see eco-camp thing!" Sami shouted.

"No!" I blurted out. They couldn't go inside. It would blow the whole thing.

"It would show our independence if we go in on our own, Mother," Sanj said calmly.

"Yeah, that," I added. "And it totally wouldn't look cool if our moms came in too."

My mom ruffled my hair.

"Oh, and that cat-sitting company that's looking after Fang while you're gone e-mailed to confirm she's OK. Strange name for a cat sitter, isn't it?" she added. "'Completely-Real-and-Not-a-Fake-Place-at-All-to-Leave-Your-Sidekick-Pets "R" Us'?"

"Umm . . . they're a chain," I said. "I think they're from out of state."

"Oh," Mom said, and lifted my backpack out of the trunk.

Phew. We were getting away with things so far.

Then I saw her arms bend in slow-mo as she went to chuck the bag on the ground and get out Sanj's pack.

"Noooooooooo!" I shouted, and threw myself at the ground so the backpack hit me instead of the dirt. I could hear a muffled "reooooowww" as I rolled with the pack and stood up. That was a close one. "I . . . um . . . don't wanna get my bag scuffed, Mom," I mumbled.

Sanj grabbed his bag, and we both managed to get through the gates with only three hair tousles, one big cheek kiss from Sanj's mom and a high five from Sami. Could have been a lot worse. And I don't think anyone clocked that my superdive for the backpack had anything to do with Fang. She was quiet again—for now.

"Mark," Sanj said as we joined the line of kids in front of the sign-in table, "did you remember to bring the Evil Plans Notebook?"

"Yep. This thing is gonna win us every contest at this place," I said, pulling the book out of my backpack. "We've got some epic evil plans."

"Let me see it again," Sanj said, snatching the book. Just as I was about to snatch it back, the person behind the desk handed us each a clipboard with a form to fill out.

As I stared at my form, wondering why they needed to know my "next of kin," I heard a voice I totally didn't expect to hear.

"Hi . . . um, I'm looking for the Eco-Scientist Camp?" a girl's voice asked. "Oh, and where is the nearest plug? I gotta charge my gear."

I looked up to see a giant backpack, with a shortish girl underneath it, stumbling through the gates.

"It can't be," I said, my mouth dropping open.

"Isn't that the irritating computer-hacking girl who helped our annoying brothers completely ruin my . . . I mean, *our* plans to use the Nicifying Helpful Minion Ray on all the neighborhood animals to make a superpet slave army?" Sanj asked. "I never forget a face . . ."

A small serious-looking budgie flew overhead and landed on a branch near the girl.

". . . or a budgie."

"It's a levitating budgie apparently," I corrected.

"It's a bird. That means it can fly, stupid," Sanj sneered.

I hated when Sanj did that. Just because he had, like, extra completely unnecessary smarts that totally got in the way sometimes, he thought everyone else was stupid. It really pushed my DEFCON-red button. My hand clenched into a ball. "I'm not stupid."

Sanj nodded. "Of course not. Silly me."

I relaxed my hand. "But, yeah, you're right, that's her. Geeky Girl."

"Geeky Girl?" Sanj repeated louder, so the other kids could hear. "What a ridiculous name."

"It's better than her real name," I started to say. "I think her name is . . ."

"Don't even . . . ," Geeky Girl said, turning toward us, heaving her backpack to the ground. "Oh, brother, it's you two!"

"Both brothers to be more accurate," Sanj corrected. "Well, welcome, Geeky Girl. We hope you enjoy your 'Eco-Scientist Camp.'"

The other kids in the sign-in line started giggling. There was a lot of mwhaa-haa-haa-haa-ing going on.

Geeky Girl looked around. "OK, something is not right here. And I know I spend a lot of time thinking that there is some conspiracy that everyone else knows and is keeping from me, but seriously, what is going on?"

I stepped up to her. "You are at the wrong

camp. Call your mom and get her to come and get you."

"My mom booked me onto this Eco-Scientist Camp for the whole break. She's gone to see my Gran in Tahiti," Geeky Girl said. "And what are you talking about? This can't be the wrong camp—"

"Oh, yes it can, my dear," Sanj interrupted. "You don't belong here. Look around."

Geeky Girl stepped up to Sanj. "You are not even starting to say that a girl can't be at this Eco-Scientist Camp, right? Because I would have to convince you otherwise." She stared him down, and he totally flinched first.

OK, I admit I liked that bit. Just to see Sanj slightly pull back from her was kinda cool.

Geeky Girl looked around and saw that there were plenty of girls in the sign-in line.

"Don't be absurd. I mean, you are the wrong type of person. Boy or girl," Sanj said. "There is no eco camp." He handed Geeky Girl the clipboard with the sign-in sheet.

CAMP MWHAAA-HAA-HA-A-WATHA
EVIL SCIENTIST SUMMER CAMP

Welcome, Campers!!!

Please sign in with your evil camp leaders, who will assign you to a tent. Stow your belongings in your tents, and you will be put into evil teams at the campfire tonight.

Evil plans at the ready.

Evil schemes encouraged.

Overt niceness will not be tolerated.

REMINDER: Absolutely no pets!!!!

_____   _____

_____   _____

_____   _____

_____   _____

3

The group of kids all mwhaa-haa-haa-ed again, as if on cue. Except Sanj only managed his usual evil wheeze that sounded like a slightly ticked-off seal.

"OK, that was kinda creepy," Geeky Girl said.

"Like I said, you need to go home," I said.

Geeky Girl folded her arms and let a smile stretch across her normally serious-looking mouth. "I'm not going anywhere. Looks like there'll be lots to check out here." She tapped her bag of computer gadgets.

No way was I going to let some friend of my little brother's ruin my summer here.

Geeky Girl had to go.

"I wouldn't miss this for a trip to Tahiti," she added.

"Seriously?" I asked, because, as cool as Evil Scientist Summer Camp was, Tahiti was well, ya know, Tahiti.

"OK, maybe I would, but Mom already left, so I'm stuck here. Might as well make the best of it. I guess I better start trying to fit in a bit around here. When in Rome . . ."

"I think we're probably in Franklin County actually."

"It's an expression." She rolled her eyes, then let out a pretty decent "Mwhaaa-haaa-haaa." It was totally better than Sanj's laugh, but not better than mine.

She dragged her pack over and got in line behind me.

"What are you doing?" I whispered. "That's it! I'm so telling the other kids that you're not really evil."

"No, you won't." She smiled.

"Yeah, I will. I'm evil like that. Remember?"

"No, you won't, because if you tell on me, then I'll tell the camp people that you brought Fang." She crossed her arms and smiled a slightly evil smile.

"B-but, I don't have Fang," I lied.

"So whose tail is that sticking out of your backpack?"

I grabbed the backpack and pulled it around to my front. A furry gray tail was flicking out of the zipper on the side of the bag. "Seriously?!" I groaned as I tucked the tail in. "Ummmm." I paused. "It's a lucky key ring."

Geeky Girl uncrossed her arms and looked smugger than a smug thing that just won a smug contest. "A key ring that purrs?" she added.

I *shhhhhh*ed my bag.

"I saw Fang peek out when I got here. She must have smelled Boris," Geeky Girl said. "And don't even think that you can tell on Boris. He can just fly away and blend into his surroundings. No one will know he's my pet."

Boris the budgie stayed on the tree branch and nodded. He looked like it was perfectly normal that there would be a budgie on a pine tree in the mountains on a regular summer's day, and that he had nothing to do with Geeky Girl. That was one cool budgie.

Just then, there was shouting at the front of the line. "I said, open your bag. Random pet check," a camp counselor said.

A kid at the front of the line with a baseball cap was bending over to open up his bag. "Sure. There's nothing in there. Certainly no pets . . . ," he started to say when the counselor knocked the kid's hat off his head. I couldn't see right away exactly what was in there, but the gasp from the rest of the campers made me pretty sure it must have been a smuggled pet.

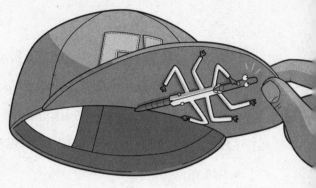

"Aha!" the counselor said. "I thought I saw that hat move." He held up the baseball hat, and I could see a stick insect wearing a little white coat clinging to the brim.

"So this isn't a pet, then?" the counselor asked the now-shaking kid.

"Ummmm, no . . . Ummm, it's a woodland animal that must have innocently climbed inside my hat when it was on the ground. Easy mistake to make. I'll just scoop him . . . I mean, IT. Scoop IT up and take it home . . . I mean, back to the woods. Right, the woods."

"So you won't mind if we just swat it right now, then?" the counselor said. There was a sucking in of breath from the campers as the counselor raised his hand to swat the insect.

He was gonna do it. I could feel Fang shaking a bit in the backpack, and I gripped it tight.

"Noooo, not Dr. Sticky!" the boy yelled as the counselor started to bring down his hand.

"Gotcha!" said the counselor, shaking his head. "There's always one that thinks they can sneak in a pet."

The boy scooped up Dr. Sticky and put him back in his hat. Two other camp counselors came up on either side of him and lifted him out of line.

"Call his parents and tell them they can collect him from the I-Stupidly-Tried-to-Break-the-Evil-Rules-and-Smuggle-in-a-Pet Stockade. Take him away. Next," the counselor behind the desk shouted after him.

I looked down at my backpack and then I looked over at Geeky Girl.

"You don't say a word about Fang or . . . ," I trailed off.

"I won't. If

you don't tell on me. So we have a deal?" She held out her hand for me to shake.

"There's no sweat truth serum, power-sucking chemical rub or itching powder on your hand, is there?" I asked. "You gotta watch your back here, you know."

"Nothing is on my hand. Now do we have a deal?"

We shook hands for like half a second just as Sanj came up to us. "Oh, how charming. You're welcoming the Geeky Girl into our evil fold." He sneered. "Well, I'm not going to let your presence ruin our plans," he said to her. "I'll tell the camp counselors that there's been a mistake with your booking, and they'll send you home where you belong. . . ."

Geeky Girl didn't even look at Sanj. She fiddled with her phone, and then played a video, tilting the screen so he could see.

My voice came out of the speaker, "Your stupid plans always go wrong!"

Then Sanj, "You can't even think up a stupid plan!"

I looked at the screen. We were both trapped

under the net in Sanj's parents' garage with a blue-footed booby sitting on top of us and Fang clamped onto Sanj's nose.

"Argh!" he screamed on the video.

"Turn that off now!" Sanj screeched in real life.

Geeky Girl hit pause.

"You say anything and I'll show this to everyone. The whole camp would love to see it. Don't you think?"

It was then that I realized there was a bit of evil in this girl after all. She might just fit in here . . . or she might seriously get in my way. Either one wasn't good. I didn't want the competition, and I definitely didn't want the hassle.

"Fine," Sanj huffed. "But this isn't the last you've heard from me."

"Ooooh, did they teach you to say that in the Evil-Comeback-Lines course in camp?" she said.

"It was an online course actually. . . ." Sanj paused—"Urgh!!!!!"—and stormed off.

"Just so you know, Geeky Girl"—I shook my head and followed after Sanj—"you are in the wrong place to be making enemies."

4

TOP FIVE THINGS I DIDN'T EXPECT ABOUT THE TENTS AT EVIL SCIENTIST SUMMER CAMP . . .

5. That I wouldn't be in a tent with Sanj (the only other human I know here besides Geeky Girl, and there's no way I want to share a tent with a girl!).

4. That the three other guys in my tent would seem to think that evil is as evil smells. Yuck.

3. That Fang would have to stay hidden in my backpack for so long. I swear she is going to burst out of it Hulk-style any minute. But at

least there were no more "random bag checks for pets." Fang is safe, but not very happy.

2. That the mosquitoes would have moved into the tent first. The bugs are taking evil to a whole new level.

And 1. That my awesomely evil summer might not be going to plan already. . . .

Once we filled out all our forms, we were given our tent numbers. Sanj was put in Tent Five at the top of the hill, and I was in Tent Two at the bottom. There were three other evil campers in my tent—Igor, Diablo and Bob—and they all knew one another from last year. They had even been Evil Scientist pen pals since then.

Bob started sneezing as soon as we got into the tent.

"Arrrchooo." He let one loose.

"Do you have hay fever or something, man?" Diablo asked.

"No, and nothing made me sneeze last year. It must be something new in the tent," Bob said, looking around, his eyes lingering on me.

I shoved my backpack with Fang still inside under my bunk. "Maybe there are, like, feathers in the pillows or something?"

"Or maybe I'm allergic to you, new kid." Bob walked up to my bunk.

I heard the sound of a kitten claw tearing through backpack as Bob stood over me.

"Ahhhhemmm," I cleared my throat to cover the sound of the bag ripping and blocked her claw with my left foot as she tried to swipe at Bob from under the bed. "Maybe it's dust?"

I shoved the backpack farther under with my foot and stood up. "We should head out to the campfire, right?"

"Urrrrghh," Igor grunted.

"Yeah, man, let's go," Diablo added.

"See you at the campfire, new kid," Bob said, and stepped back just as another claw swipe missed his leg. They headed out of the tent, and I dropped down on my knees by my bunk and yanked out the backpack, with an angry kitten half in and half out.

"Well, that was way smart, Fang," I said as I unzipped the pack and let her jump free. "If they find you, they'll turn you in."

"Meooooow." Fang tossed her head back like she didn't care who heard her. I muffled her with an Evil Scientist Summer Camp baseball hat just as Igor popped his head back through the tent flaps.

"Urgh?"

"Yeah, I heard something too," I said. "I think it was outside."

"Urgh." He nodded and headed out again.

I lifted off the cap and smoothed back Fang's fur.

"'Reooow,' she meow-whispered.

"I know you wanna swipe that Bob guy," I said as she curled around my legs. "I wanna swipe him too. But I've got to try to build up a posse around here. They are the kids I need to win over if Sanj and I are going to make the most of camp and out-evil the other evil kids. If we win the first competition, we get the Evil Emperor of the Week crown, which we totally will with all our evil plans. Plus we get points toward the final Evil Kid of the Summer Prize. Last year that kid got a whole article about her in *Evil Scientist* magazine!"

Fang head-butted my arm and let me stroke her once before she headed back under the bed.

"Right, stay outta sight until I'm back from the campfire. I'll bring you something to eat."

"Meooow."

"Yeah, maybe I might be lucky and find a bird. Maybe a budgie?" I laughed my best "Mwhaaa-haaa-haa-a-haaa."

5

When I got to the campfire, most of the seats on the logs surrounding the fire were taken.

There was a group of cool and deadly-looking evil girls on one of the logs. There was the log with the evil Goth kids, one for the evil sporty kids, one for the evil brainy kids and then a log that had just Bob, Diablo and Igor on it. To be fair, Igor takes up a lot of log.

Sanj was sitting on a log with a space next to him. But this tall kid with amazingly bouncy hair, I mean like hair-shampoo-commercial-level bouncy hair, strode over and sat in the seat. Sanj smiled over at me and shrugged his shoulders.

There was one log left, and guess who was sitting on it all on her own with nothing but a serious-looking budgie sitting on the branch above it.

Geeky Girl.

"This does not mean I want to sit here," I said as I walked over. "This does not mean that I even want to breathe the same air or whatever as you."

"Why are you even talking?" She glared at me. "Argh. This is just like school."

"This is nothing like school," I said. "First, at school, well, there isn't a giant fire—not usually anyway—but second, there is no way I would sit on my own or sit with you. I would slide kids off a log if I wanted to sit on it. If they had logs in the cafeteria, which they don't."

"OK, your mouth is still moving." She rolled her eyes.

"Well, HELLO THERE, EVIL CAMPERS!!! Welcome to Camp Mwhaaa-haa-ha-a-watha!" a really loud cheerleader-type voice boomed from the center of the circle.

"Mwhaaa-haa-ha-a-watha!" the kids all chanted back in unison.

"No, this isn't 'culty' at all?" Geeky Girl mumbled.

I looked at the center of the circle, and there was the full team of Evil Scientist Summer Camp leaders—just like on the website.

"Who are these people?" Geeky Girl whispered.

"That is Kirsty Katastrophe!" I paused. "With a *K*," I added. Still no response. Geeky Girl obviously had no idea about the celebrity status of any of these camp leaders. How could anyone be soooooo out of touch?

"She was Young Evil Scientist of the Year last year and was responsible for a hypnotic cheer at a university football game that immobilized an entire stadium of people!"

I could feel my voice getting higher and higher as I told Geeky Girl about Kirsty Katastrophe's awesome evilness. "So she's pretty evil. You know, not bad. I mean bad, but not bad at being bad . . . um . . . you know what I mean."

I was saved by Kirsty Katastrophe shouting out again, "And what do we do at Camp Mwhaaa-haa-ha-a-watha?"

"We live, breathe and sweat Evil Science!!!" all the kids replied.

"Ewwww," Geeky Girl whispered, crinkling up

her nose. She looked at the rest of the leaders. "So who are the other ones?"

"The tall guy next to her is Trevor the Tech-in-ator," I whispered back.

"The what?" she said.

"The clue is in the name. Ya know, like a terminator with tech?" I said.

"Hey, is he the guy who crashed the whole public-school computer system of Switzerland with a malware that made all the computers yodel?" Geeky Girl suddenly looked interested. "He's a legend in hacking circles."

"I always thought that stunt was kinda . . . obvious," I said, pushing some dirt with a stick I'd picked up from the ground. "The other shorter guy is Phillipe Fortescue. He's a master of evil disguise."

Geeky Girl stared at the unassuming, mousy-haired man with a wiry mustache. "Him?"

"He is epic," I said. "I heard he once smuggled himself out of a museum that he'd just robbed by posing as a piece of modern art that was being saved from the robbery." My voice started to get a little high again from the excitement. "So he's not bad either." I paused again. "But in a bad way." I had lowered my voice back to its normal cool, I-don't-really-care-about-much tone.

"Now let's all sing the Camp Mwhaaa-haa-ha-a-watha song," Kirsty Katastrophe called out. Most of the kids seemed to already know the words.

"CAMP MWHAAA-HAA-HA-A-WATHA
WE SING TO YOU
WE HOPE OUR E-VIL PLANS COME TRUE
ASIDE LAKE DASTARDLY YOU'RE SAT
AWAY FROM ANY DOG OR CAT
WE'LL TOIL AND STRIVE ALL SUMMER LONG
TO COME UP WITH A SLIGHTLY EVILER SONG."

"Yeah, they could totally do with way better lyrics," I said.

Geeky Girl nodded. "This is going to be a looooong summer."

6

"Thank you, campers!" Kirsty shouted.

Everyone Mwahhaaa-haa-haa-ed back at her.

"Trevor, Phillipe and I would like to welcome you to Evil Scientist Summer Camp."

"Yaaa, velcome," Trevor droned in a deep gravelly voice.

"Happy to see so many of the same evil faces back with us again," Phillipe added.

"OK," Kirsty chirped, "so we hope you've settled into your tents. Now, for those of you who are new to Evil Scientist Summer Camp ... can we just have a show of hands here to see who that is?"

I raised my hand. Geeky Girl slightly raised an arm stuck up a sweater sleeve so no actual hand was shown. Sanj raised his hand, and the bouncy hair guy next to him held up his hand too.

"Wonderful," Kirsty said. "In a bit we'll get everyone into their pairs for the first week's project, Evil Traps. The winners of this week's contest will become Evil Emperors of the Week."

"Wicked." I punched the air. "I am soooo good at evil traps." I elbowed Geeky Girl. "And Sanj and I already planned out, like, a bunch of them in our Evil Plans Notebook." I patted my jacket pocket. It wasn't there. I never got it back from Sanj. Then I smelled the slightly scorched hot dogs and my stomach rumbled a totally evil rumble. I could get the book off Sanj after dinner.

"You can't make evil plans on an empty stomach," I said to Geeky Girl.

The rest of the campfire went by in a bit of a blur. We sang one more blast of the not-so-evil-really camp song and had some not-so-evil hot dogs, and then Kirsty started talking again.

"Right, we'll all meet up at the lake tomorrow morning. We'll have a session on evil getaways, with speedboat practice after that, and then you'll get some time to work in your pairs on your evil traps. Remember, the worst team will be sent home on the Canoe of Shame."

There was a general murmur of "Mwhaaa-haa-haa" and "Ohhh no, not the Canoe of Shame" from the other campers.

Geeky Girl raised her hand. "Umm, seriously, did you just say the 'Canoe of Shame'?"

Kirsty put her hands on her hips and nodded. "Yes, that's exactly what I said."

"So, basically, are we talking an actual canoe, or is this a metaphor for something more evil?" Geeky Girl asked.

She was not getting in good with the counselors here.

Trevor the Tech-in-ator then reached down behind a log and pulled up a canoe with a big sign on it that said "SHAME." On the other side it said "property of Camp Mwhaaa-haa-ha-a-watha."

"I think that's more of a kayak actually," I heard Bouncy Hair Guy mumble.

"Yes, it's
the seat position
that distinguishes ...,"
Sanj agreed before he was *shhh*ed by Kirsty.

"It's the 'CANOE of Shame,' and you don't want to be on the 'Canoe of Shame' at the end of the week, do you?" she huffed.

The campers all called out "Nooooo!" together.

"On the other hand, if you win, you will be crowned Evil Emperor of the Week." She smiled a brilliantly evil smile.

I wanted that evil crown. I was picturing everyone bowing and calling me "Evil King Mark," when Geeky Girl elbowed me again. "They don't give you a real crown, do they? That would be tacky. It's probably just a certificate or something."

That totally ruined my daydream. It's hard to picture people bowing to you when you're wearing an evil certificate.

Kirsty Katastrophe spoke to us again. "Now let's move on to your mantra of the day," she said, looking directly at Geeky Girl and me. "These are very important to learn, especially if you are new to Evil Scientist Summer Camp."

"In every day and every way, I'm getting eviler and eviler—"

"Excuse me, camp leader," Sanj interrupted. "Wouldn't it be more correct to say . . . 'I'm getting more and more evil'?"

Kirsty's left eyebrow arched and she glared at Sanj, but kept her perfect cheerleader smile switched on the whole time. "No." She leaned over him. "And it would not be as catchy."

"Like I said before, not a good place to make enemies," I whispered to Geeky Girl. "Especially important enemies like that." I looked over at Kirsty, who was still eyeballing Sanj as she spoke.

"It's time to choose your teams for the first evil contest. Are you ready?"

The campers all let out a loud "Mwhaa-haaa-haaa-haaa" together.

"So what happens now?" Geeky Girl called out. "Do you have an Evil Scientist version of a sorting hat? Are we assessed and assigned a partner based on evil compatibility? This is going to be really exciting, right?"

Trevor looked menacingly around the fire, then just shrugged, and said, "Everyone pick someone to work with on this one."

"What? Is that it?" Geeky Girl stood up as all the other kids paired off.

I looked over to Sanj, where I spotted him fist-bump the kid with the hair.

Phillipe glared at Geeky Girl and me. "I suppose that means the two of you will be working together." He smiled. "Hmmmmm . . ."

"No, I mean, I was gonna work with Sanj. Right, Sanj?" I called desperately.

Sanj just looked over at me, and said, "Terribly sorry. Dustin asked me first."

"Dustin?!" I scoffed. Then Sanj pulled our Evil Plans Notebook out of his pocket. He whispered something to Dustin and they fist-bumped again.

"You have to have a partner," Phillipe interrupted. "Or would you like me to call your parents and send you home?"

The other kids all Mwhaaa-haa-haa-giggled (which is pretty hard to do. They must practice).

"So, what will it be? Partner with . . . What was your name again?" Phillipe asked.

"Geeky Girl."

"Really? . . . Well, with her?" Phillipe added. "Or go home?"

"We'll work together," Geeky Girl said, and elbowed me in the ribs.

"Owwww," I said. "I mean, OK."

Everyone started chatting with their new partners, but I was not in the mood.

I got up and stuffed a couple more hot dogs into my sweatshirt for Fang.

I would show them. I'd totally win the evil trap

contest. I'd totally beat Sanj and what's-his-name, and I'd get that stupid Evil Emperor of the Week crown . . . somehow.

I mwhaaa-haa-haa-ed to myself. I thought it would make me feel a bit better, but instead, it just made me look like a kid who went around mwhaaa-ha-haaa-ing to myself.

"Now," Trevor's voice boomed across the flames of the dying campfire, "you can all take zee marshmallow to toast at zee edge of zee fire." And he opened up a Tupperware container of marshmallows on sticks. "Come and get zhem."

I didn't feel like toasting marshmallows—felt more like toasting Sanj—so I stomped over to him and the hair kid, who had already grabbed a marshmallow stick.

"Mark," Sanj said. "Let me introduce Dustin."

The kid turned around and tossed his hair to the side. It bounced exactly into place. It was spooky.

"How's it goin'?" Dustin said, and tossed his hair effortlessly to the other side.

"Bad," I said, and then blanked him and talked to Sanj.

"What's with the kid with the hair?" I asked.

"Dustin," Sanj corrected.

"Whatever," I continued. "We had stuff planned. We were gonna work together. We had ideas. . . ."

"I just had to seize the moment, Mark," Sanj said. "Besides, Dustin has some great trap ideas too. He's actually been out in the wild and trapped things." Then he lowered his voice. "He's Canadian, you know."

"And he's evil?" I said. "No way."

"Um, that's like a major national stereotype, dude," Dustin jumped in. "I'm evil and I'm Canadian and I'm proud of it." Then he paused. "Oh, excuse me for interrupting."

Was this guy for real?

"Fine!" I said to Sanj. "I hope you and the Canadian trapper dude are happy together." I held out my hand. "I just want my notebook back."

"I don't have it," Sanj said, but I knew he was lying.

"Look, I can turn you upside down and shake it out of you, or you can hand it to me." I stepped toward him.

But Dustin crossed between us. "I think you should leave it. We aren't allowed any unauthorized violence at camp," he said.

"This is an EVIL Scientist Camp and it's against the rules to thump somebody?" I said.

"Yes. You can thump people during Evil Henchmen 101, but not outside class." Dustin tossed his hair again. "I checked the rules very carefully."

I couldn't believe there were that many rules at an EVIL camp that you had to check.

"I will get that book, Sanj," I said. "Those are my ideas too and you can't steal them. And I'll build a better trap than you losers anyway. Even if I have to work with a waste of space like Geeky Girl."

I turned to stomp off when I bumped directly into Geeky Girl.

She did not give me any size smile this time. What she did give me was a totally evil glare.

"You aren't my first choice either, you . . ." She let her evil glare look me up and down as she decided how to insult me. ". . . you . . . you . . . wall!" She didn't seem happy with that insult at all, and she looked like she was gonna kick me in the shins instead, but Dustin tutted at her.

"Tut, tut, tut . . . unauthorized violence." He shook his head.

So instead she walked over and mashed his marshmallow right in his face. Then she stormed away.

"I bet that takes ages to wash out of bangs," I said as I walked off, just hearing Dustin mumble, "I'm sure that counts as unauthorized violence."

Geeky Girl strode off into her tent, and I swear she slammed the tent flap. I didn't think that was even possible.

I kinda thought I should maybe try to say sorry for the line about her being a waste of space. I was mad at Sanj, not her. I thought maybe I should say something at least, but just as I passed my tent, I stopped.

From inside, I could hear a very low *hisssss*.

"It's a snake, man!" I could hear Diablo shouting. "There's a snake in here."

8

I recognized that hiss. Not that I've heard many snake hisses in my time. Well, none in real life to be exact and only a couple in movies. But this hiss I'd heard all the time. This was pretty specific. It was a clear, I'm-really-mad-that-I-can't-go-out-and-I'm-hungry-and-I-haven't-bitten-anything-in-a-really-long-time hiss. And I knew exactly who was making it.

I pulled back the tent flaps to find Diablo, Bob and Igor all standing on Igor's bed, trying to poke a stick under my bed. I strode up to my bed and stood there.

"What's the deal?" I asked.

"Get back, man," Diablo shouted. "There's a snake under there!"

"And it doesn't sound happy," Bob added.

"Urrrggghh!" Igor agreed.

"Is that it?" I smiled and reached out and grabbed the stick from Diablo.

"Well, that snake picked the wrong bed to hide under," I said, pushing up the sleeves of my white Evil Scientist coat.

"Can you get it out?" Bob asked.

"That snake is gonna wish he'd never met Mark the Snake-in-ator," I added.

"Is that your name?" Bob asked.

"Well, the Snake-in-ator bit is really a tag, ya know . . . ," I started.

"No, Mark. I just call you Annoying New Kid—"

"Or just New Kid if you're in a good mood, Bob," Diablo interrupted.

"Yeah," Bob said.

I didn't realize they thought I was annoying. Me? How? I mean, I just thought they were hanging back and being cool about accepting me. I had to ramp up the action and get them on my side.

A louder hiss came from under the bed, and they all jumped back even farther onto Igor's bed.

"I'll handle this," I said smugly. 'Cause, really, how else can you say a line like that at a time like this?

"What are you going to do to it when you get it?" Diablo asked.

"Do you wanna see?" I said, and started poking under the bed with the stick. The hissing got louder.

"Noooo," Bob and Diablo shouted together, while Igor made a slightly higher-pitched "Urgh." Then the three of them bolted out of the tent, leaving me alone with the stick and the monster under the bed.

"You can come out now, Fang," I whispered,

pulling the campfire hot dogs out of my pocket
and holding them out to her.

The hiss turned into a low *grrrrrrowl* as she
smelled dinner.

Fang poked out a single claw and swiped one
of the hot dogs and pulled it under the bed. Then,
after a few seconds of gobbling noises, she came
out purring.

She rubbed up against my knees as I knelt next
to the bed. "We got them good, didn't we, kitten?"
I said as I stroked her ears.

She rose up and kitten fist-bumped me and
then, just cause she's Fang, she swiped my hand
with her claw.

"Owww!" I pulled back. "You are definitely
more dangerous than a snake."

Fang purred and then grabbed the second hot dog and dove back under the bed just as Bob peeked into the tent.

"We heard you yell," he said. "Did the snake get you?"

"Just a nip," I said, letting him see the blood on my hand from the scratch. "No big thing. I got him cornered. Won't be long now."

Bob ducked back out of the tent, and I could hear him telling the other guys how the snake bit me but I kept fighting it.

"They'll be so embarrassed when they find out they were scared of a little kitten, won't they, Fang?" I whispered. Then it hit me. They could never know. Apart from the fact that me and Fang would be thrown out of camp, they'd know I'd been lying about the snake, and I would go from potential Snake-in-ator kid to Annoying-camper-who-made-up-that-he-fought-a-snake kid. They had to think Fang was a snake.

I reached under the bed and took the hot dog away from Fang. She immediately hissed at me.

I thumped against the underside of the bed and shouted, "I'll get you, snake!" and then I added a loud "You're no match for me!" because at the time it sounded like an I'm-fighting-an-imaginary-snake kind of thing to say. Fang looked at me like my head had just fallen off. "Come on, kitten, play along," I whispered. "I have to make this sound good."

I took another hot dog out of my pocket and waved it in front of Fang, but wouldn't give it to her. She hissed and swiped at it.

I could hear Bob and the guys outside the tent. "Man, that snake is fighting back."

"Maybe he can't defeat it?" Diablo said.

I was rolling around under the bed, making as much pretend fighting noise as possible, while occasionally letting Fang get a bite of hot dog

so she wouldn't actually lose her cool, when a moment of pure genius happened. Ya know when you're just doing some ordinary mundane evil thing and you suddenly have an evil lightbulb go off in your head? That happened. Evil genius can show itself in unexpected ways, and mine showed when I rolled over on a ketchup packet.

I suddenly knew how I was going to convince them that I'd killed the snake. Ketchup blood! I took the remaining hot dogs out of my pocket and stuck them on the stick. Then I rolled them in the smeared ketchup that was on the floor from the squashed packet. Fang licked up the rest of the ketchup while I wrapped up the "snake" in a T-shirt and—boom!—instant dead, defeated snake body on a stick!

I made some final snake-fighting noises and
then went quiet.

"OK, Fang, here's the last hot dog. Stay curled
up under here, and I'll be back in a bit. *Shhhh.*"

She meowed, licked more ketchup off my
fingers and slunk back under the bed to snooze.

I stood up and strode over to the tent flap,
whipping it back dramatically and stepping outside.

"Is that . . . it?" Bob said, staring at the "bloody"-
T-shirt-covered mess I was carrying.

"Yup." I shrugged. "All that snake wrestling
got me hungry. I'm just gonna go cook this on the
campfire. Anyone else want BBQ snake?"

The guys all shook their heads and then took a
step back and let me pass.

Now this was how I thought camp was going to be.

I didn't need Sanj, and I didn't need Geeky Girl.
I got respect from some hot dogs and ketchup in a
T-shirt. Result!

I could hear them mumbling, "Mark the Snake-
in-ator" as I walked away.

I woke up the next morning to the sound of a trumpet.

"Dum, Dum, Dum, da da Dum, da da Dum!"

"Darth Vader music?" I mumbled from under the covers.

"It was the evilest thing the kid with the trumpet knows," Bob said.

"He's playing it better than last year," Diablo said.

I looked at my watch. Six a.m.!

I guess ya gotta start early in evil camp.

I got up and pulled on a T-shirt, sweatshirt and shorts and started to put on my white coat.

"Urgghh." Igor shook his head at me.

"We'll be doing throws into the lake this

morning. You don't need your white coat, New K—" Bob stopped himself. "Mark."

I quickly pulled on my swim shorts instead and threw the white coat on the bed.

"Let's get going," Diablo said, and raced out of the tent. I followed the rest, and then remembered Fang. "Um, guys, I'll catch you at the lake. I gotta ... umm ... umm ... umm ... fold my white coat." They turned around.

"Seriously?" Bob asked.

"Hey, man, respect the white coat, and it will respect you," Diablo said.

"Urgh," Igor nodded.

"Yeah, so I'll see you guys in a bit," I mumbled as I dove back inside the tent.

"Pssst, Fang," I whispered. A few seconds later Fang stretched her front half out from under the bed, arched her back and then slowly walked her back half up to meet her front.

"I'm going down to the lake, but I'll bring you back something from breakfast after." She purred and rubbed against my leg. "Just stay put."

I ran out and caught up with the guys on the pier by the lake. Sanj and Dustin were there already. They had that look like they were already well into planning evil stuff together. I recognized it, because Sanj and I were like that when we were plotting evil stuff. Geeky Girl was standing on her own in a proper wet suit. She didn't even make a corner-of-eye contact with me.

"We have a lot of evil stuff to cover this morning, so we're going to kick off right away," Kirsty Katastrophe said. Then she leaned back and karate-kicked the kid closest to the pier's edge into the lake.

"Aaaarrrrgggghhh," the kid spluttered, and splashed in the water.

"Lesson One: the element of surprise." She smiled as the kid pulled himself back onto the pier.

I tried to quietly stand at the back with Bob and the other guys. As I came up to them, I heard Bob say to another kid, "Then he caught it in his bare hands. It bit him, but that didn't even stop him."

Kirsty said, "Now, all of you should hope to get an apprenticeship as an evil henchman at some point."

I could see Geeky Girl rolling her eyes at this, and Sanj mumbled, "I have much higher aspirations, of course."

"You are going to need some basic skills. Blocking, chasing and throwing are the top three that you will need to master to get to your Evil Henchmen Basic, Level One," she said, walking to the end of the pier. "Now I'm going to demonstrate some throws."

She looked out into the crowd of eager campers waiting to be thrown into the cold lake by Kirsty and totally grateful for that chance. "You!" She pointed over toward Bob, Igor and Diablo. Bob stepped forward.

"No, I mean Snake Kid," she said. Bob did that thing where he looked like he hadn't meant to step forward but did a little kick with his foot, like there was a piece of dirt that needed kicking at that exact time and he needed to be the one to do it. Lame cover, really. Then he stepped back, and I stepped forward. "Me?"

She nodded and I came forward to the edge of the pier. She called me Snake Kid. She had heard of me. I was in awe.

The next five minutes were a haze of being flipped over into the water again and again by Kirsty. I probably sprained my shoulder, bruised parts of me that I didn't realize could bruise, and I still can't remember a single move that she did. But those five minutes were possibly the best five minutes of my entire life to that point.

As I climbed back up onto the pier after her final throw, I was smiling ear to ear.

"OK, go and grab some breakfast. Then we'll meet back here for some chase training on evil getaways." She slapped my arm as I wrung out the water from my T-shirt. "Nice one, Snake Kid."

I'm pretty sure that I floated back to the mess tent. By the time I got there I was starving. Being the Snake-in-ator is hard work.

I piled my plate with bacon, eggs, toast and double of everything.

"Mark!" My food piling was interrupted by the sound of Sanj's voice coming from a table on the left side of the tent. "There's a space here," he said.

I smiled as I walked over in his direction and then straight past him and Dustin to Bob's table.

"Mark? Mark?" Sanj shouted after me. "Oh, he must not have heard me." He covered, and said to the other people at his table, "We got our evil start together, you know? The Snake-in-ator and me."

I think my walking had turned into a full-on swagger by the time I brushed past Geeky Girl at the cereal counter. She wouldn't even look me in the eye, but I heard her mumble, "The Snake-in-ator? Please." I still felt kinda bad about yesterday, but there was no way I was gonna let her ruin my moment.

Bob, Igor and Diablo slid over to make room at their table, and I slammed down my tray with an evil *thwak!* "Nailed that throw, right?" I said, and fist-bumped Diablo.

"Totally evil throw," he said back. "Kirsty was impressed, man. You are on your way to this week's Emperor of the Camp."

It was then, in the glory of my most perfect morning ever of all time that I saw the furry gray tail disappearing under the flap of the mess tent and heading for the kitchen.

10

Fang! Oh no! I jumped up and looked over. Geeky Girl had spotted it too. She gave me that look that said, "You have no control over that kitten, do you? You don't see my budgie misbehaving like that." It was a very huffy look.

"Ummmm, I'm still hungry," I said. "I'm gonna go see what they have left in the kitchen," and I rushed around the side of the tent.

That's when I heard the shriek.

"There's a rat! Look, a rat!" a voice squealed from the kitchen tent. I pulled back the opening and saw the cook waving a saucepan over his head and stomping his feet on the ground. I had to get Fang outta there before she was knocked sideways with the saucepan. There was a rustling in the storage cupboard and flashes of gray fur as something jumped and rummaged through the food stores.

"I got this," I said in my same smug voice from the night before. It was totally becoming natural for me to sound this smug. It was like Mark the Snake-in-ator had a deep pay-attention-to-me voice with just a hint of "na naa naa naaa naaa" thrown in.

I got the saucepan from the cook and grabbed a lid from the counter. Then I crawled into the cupboard. Sure enough, Fang was happily clawing open a packet of sandwich meats and licking the lid of a peanut butter jar she'd managed to knock over.

"I thought you were gonna stay in the tent, Fang," I whispered. I went to scoop her into the saucepan, but she dodged me and jumped up out of reach. I raised my head to see where she went and—*thwak*—my head hit the bottom of the shelf. "Owwwwwch!" I shouted.

"Did you get it?" the cook said, trying to look over my shoulder. "I will never take a job in a campsite again!" he mumbled to himself. "I am a four-star evil chef, not a rat catcher."

"Fang, come on. If you don't let me catch you, that guy is gonna splat you with a frying pan," I whispered.

"You are talking to the rat?" the chef shouted from behind me.

"Yeah . . . umm . . . rats are really smart, so I'm explaining to the rat that it has to go, but I'll take it somewhere where there's better food." I looked at Fang when I said that bit.

"Not that your food isn't good, you know, just for rat taste . . ." I gave up trying to explain. Fang jumped down off the shelf, and as she casually licked peanut butter off her paw, I managed to sneak the saucepan behind her and scoop her inside (complete with peanut-butter-jar lid). I slammed the lid on the saucepan. "Got it!" I said.

When I crawled out of the cupboard, the cook
was wiping his brow with a dish towel. "Thank
you," he said. "Now, get that out of here. Please. I
HATE rats!"

By the time I came out of the cupboard there
was already a group of kids watching.

"Look, the Snake-in-ator kid got something
else," one of them said.

"Take it away!" the chef shouted. "Far, far
away."

I carried Fang (still licking the peanut-butter-
jar lid) in the saucepan out into the woods. I took
off the lid of the saucepan and gently emptied her
onto the grass, when I heard the voice behind me.

"That kitten is going to get you kicked out of camp in the first week." Geeky Girl shook her head and folded her arms.

"And why do you care?" I said.

"I don't care about you or Fang," she said. Fang looked up at Geeky Girl and hissed. Then went back to licking her peanut butter. "But if they find her, then the camp counselors might start looking more closely and eventually find Boris too."

"You worry about Boris, and I'll worry about Fang."

"Just keep her out of sight," Geeky Girl said. She looked at her watch. "We're going to be late for Evil Getaway practice."

"No one is stopping you," I said.

She looked around. "Look, you can't expect a kitten to stay hidden. You shouldn't have brought her, but since you did, you're going to have to find someplace safe to keep her."

She turned to walk away. "I might have an idea."

I picked up Fang and the saucepan and

followed Geeky Girl farther down the path into the woods. She pointed up to her right into the trees. "Do you see it?"

I squinted through the sunlight up into the branches and saw what looked like a tree house.

"Boris showed it to me this morning. I was going to use it as a non-evil hideout, but you know, if the kitten wants to stay there when I'm not there . . ."

I put Fang on the ground and pulled myself up the couple of branches into the tree house. It wasn't bad. Fang could totally hang out here. Safely up out of the way with some water and food.

Before I knew it, I felt a brush of fur against my leg. Fang had climbed up behind me.

"What do you think? An evil lair fit for an evil kitten?" I said.

"Meoooooow." She purred and curled herself around my leg.

I shouted down to Geeky Girl. "OK, she'll take it. Pass me that saucepan."

Geeky Girl handed me the saucepan, which I filled up with water from my water bottle. Then I rolled up my sweatshirt and made a bed for Fang. She clawed around it, checking it out, and then lay down.

"Do you think she'll stay there?" Geeky Girl called up.

"Fang," I said, stroking her ear, "you have to stay out of the way."

"I have to get back to practice evil getaways. I'll see you after lunch." I crouched down and looked her right in the eye. "Stay out here; don't let anyone see you." She licked her paws and rolled over.

"Good kitty," I said. Fang hissed. "I mean, evil kitty, evil, evil kitty." I scratched her just behind the ears. "Now I gotta figure out how Mark the Snake-in-ator can get that Evil Plans Notebook from Sanj. An evil plan will come to me."

"Dum, Dum, Dum, da da Dum, da da Dum," the Darth Vader trumpet sounded.

"Right. Gotta go. My fans back at camp are waiting for me. Mwwwhaaa-haaa-haaa-haaa-haa," I said, and scratched Fang on the top of her head.

"Hey, thanks for finding . . . ," I started to say as I jumped down from the tree house, but Geeky Girl was already gone.

11

I got back to the lake just in time for Trevor the Tech-in-ator's talk about hot-wiring speedboats for getaways. Then he moved on to the more advanced bit about defusing the bombs that were on the boats. This was in case the good guys you're stealing from, or some evil rival group, might have rigged the boat so it blows up if you steal it. Either way it was hot-wiring and driving a speedboat. That sounded fun.

I stopped listening to the bomb-disposal bit sometime after he said, "Never cut the red wire." There was more interesting stuff to eavesdrop on.

Diablo was talking to one of the killer Goth evil girls and kept pointing over at me. I couldn't hear everything, but I caught "totally evil hombre" and "muy grande serpiente."

"It means 'really big snake,'" Geeky Girl interrupted my eavesdropping, making me wonder if she could read my mind. "You had that trying-to-figure-it-out-and-not-having-a-clue look on your face, so I thought I would translate," she explained.

"I don't need you to translate," I lied.

"So you understand Spanish?" Geeky Girl responded.

"No, but I understand . . ."

I was just about to come back at her with a totally evil and cutting comeback that I hadn't thought of yet when Trevor the Tech-in-ator interrupted.

"If you two are talking during my demo, zhen you must know all zhere is about hot-wiring a getaway boat, defusing zee potential bomb and circling zee lake to escape your enemies? Right?"

"Ummmmm?" I said. There had to be some way to get out of this. I was the Snake-in-ator, right? That must count for something.

"Sorry, we were ummm . . . ," Geeky Girl started.

"So come up here and demonstrate, then," Trevor said, and stepped back from the boat.

"Both of us? 'Cause she was really talking more . . . ," I said.

"Both," he barked. "Now."

We both shuffled forward and looked at the boat. It actually looked a bit like a boat I had driven in the water-sports activity center a few months before.

"I think I can drive it," I whispered to Geeky Girl. "If you can do the bomb?"

She nodded and looked over at Trevor. "Are we being timed?"

"The clock started vhen I said 'now,'" he said, and smiled a really evil smile. I mean, that man could patent that evil smile. "You have three minutes."

Geeky Girl huffed, jumped into the boat and started working on the pretend bomb. At least I hoped it was a pretend bomb.

I jumped into the boat too and went to the front.

"You have to hot-wire zee boat first to get it to start," Trevor shouted to me.

"Not when you have a universal getaway starting key that works on almost all getaway boats, cars and motorcycles," I said. "Ninteen ninety-nine plus twenty *Evil Scientist* magazine coupons in the last issue." I pulled it out of my pocket and started up the engine.

"That's cheating," Trevor shouted back. "Extra points for cheating. Vell done," he added, and wrote something down in his notebook.

As we sped away out into the water, I could hear Sanj back on the pier saying, "So that's where all my *Evil Scientist* magazine coupons went!"

My mind started to wander a bit as I drove the boat.

They wouldn't let a bunch of kids practice on a real bomb, right?

But we did have to sign that next-of-kin form. . . .

My wandering mind was brought back to the boat with a bump. Literally.

"Hey!" Geeky Girl shouted from the back of the boat. "You think you could not make the boat jump every wave? Defusing a pretend bomb here. A little less bumping would be nice."

"So you're sure it's a pretend bomb, right?" I said. "It is EVIL Scientist Camp."

"So you think it might be real and you're still going over bumps?" Geeky Girl added.

"Right," I said. "I'm on it." And then one of the

kids on the pier waved to me as I circled past again and crossed over the wake from my own boat. "Whooooaaaa."

I could feel the boat surge up at the front and come down with a slam at the back. I looked over my shoulder to see Geeky Girl flipped up into the air by the force of the wave. She was heading overboard!

12

"Got ya!" I shouted, and reached back and grabbed Geeky Girl's backpack before she was bounced out of the boat.

"So that is LESS bouncing?" she said.

"I am re-creating authentic getaway conditions," I said. "So there. People would be chasing us, and chasing sometimes involves bumps."

She mumbled something at me, but I couldn't make it out. Actually, I wasn't sure I wanted to.

I waited a few seconds and then shouted again over the roar of the engine, "How's that bomb going, Geeky Girl?"

"Nearly done. I think," she mumbled. "I hope this works."

I wished that she sounded surer.

We headed back to the pier, having circled the lake, and jumped out of the boat just as Trevor clicked his stopwatch.

"Made it!" I shouted, and punched the air.

"Just," said Trevor. "And did you manage to defuse ze bomb? Who vould like to check?"

Sanj strode forward. "I'm a wiz at all tech devices. I could have defused that bomb in my sleep. I'll check out the shoddy work of this amateur," Sanj said, and stepped up on the deck of the boat.

"Sanj, I think you'll want to check . . . ," Geeky Girl said.

"I don't think I need advice from you," Sanj sneered, pushing past Geeky Girl.

She stepped off the boat, folded her arms and smiled. Then she started quietly counting as Sanj fiddled with the wires on the bomb.

"One evil genius, two evil genius, three evil genius," she mumbled.

"What on earth are you doing? It's distracting," Sanj started to say, when suddenly a loud siren sounded, and you could hear a recording of Geeky Girl's voice saying, "Danger, this person is planting a bomb and needs to be apprehended at once! Danger!" on a repeat loop.

Sanj staggered back from the pretend bomb, covering his ears.

"Look out!" Geeky Girl shouted over her own booming recorded voice.

But Sanj toppled right over the side of the boat and splashed into the cold lake.

Geeky Girl shook her head. "Yes, sir, I defused the bomb, but I had some extra time, so I added a fail-safe so it couldn't be reactivated again without the alarm going off."

Then she smiled a pretty evil smile, and added, "I hope that's OK?"

Sanj clambered back onto the pier, dripping as he walked, and joined the others.

"Zhis is more than OK. You can both head back with zee others now, and maybe you can give zhem some tips, as zhey'll all have a go at zhis before lunch," Trevor said.

I went back and high-fived with Bob, Diablo and Igor.

While the rest of the campers practiced their getaways, I got lots of slaps on the back and nods of "top evil getaway, dude" from some of the

guys. Geeky Girl and Trevor talked the whole time about her pretend bomb tampering. "So it's really just a simple modification of the secondary circuit that shorts out the primary detonator and circumvents the auxiliary widget."

OK, so I don't think she actually said "widget," but my brain was full with big words by then, so I stopped listening.

"It's time for lunch," Trevor announced once the last kid pulled himself out of the lake after crashing the boat into the pier. My stomach had started growling already.

When I get hungry I think more. That's kind of why I don't like to be too hungry. I don't want too much thinking to turn me into Sanj or anything. But my growling stomach did get me thinking.

Me and the guys. I liked saying that. It was always just either "me and Sanj" or "me and some kids I made do what I want," but these were guys who were choosing to hang with me. I kinda liked it. So me and the guys headed back to camp for lunch.

Trevor called after us. "Remember zhis

afternoon is set aside to work in your pairs for ze Evil Trap-Making Competition. The winning team gets named Evil Emperors of the Week and gets points toward the end-of-camp prize, Evil Emperor of the Camp."

Great. That means a whole afternoon of working with Geeky Girl. She'll be really smug about acing the bomb thing too. Although I gotta admit it was really cool to see Sanj land in the lake. But it's not fair. Bob and Diablo have been thinking of stuff since last year. Igor is just excited to be carrying evil stuff back and forth to help out the evil Goth girl he's paired with, and I'm stuck with Geeky Girl. She'll probably want to build some eco-friendly, not-even-remotely-evil trap. Plus Sanj and Dustin are probably already working on something really amazing from our notebook of evil plans. I gotta get that notebook back. I need an evil plan, and I need stealth and off-the-chart sneakiness to do it. I need Fang.

13

When we got to the mess tent, the cook was waiting for me. "I prepared my specialty to thank you for disposing of the rat this morning. Evil superburgers for you and your table." He plonked down a tray of yummy-looking burgers in front of us.

"Result! Dig in," I said as I moved the plate out of the way of the string of drool dangling out of

Igor's mouth. I gobbled down a few and pocketed one for Fang.

I looked over at Geeky Girl and Sanj eating the lunch slop casserole that was the dish of the day and smiled. This was the life. I was Mark the Snake-in-ator. I had respect. I had a posse. I had burgers.

"I'll see you later," I said as I walked out and headed down to the woods to try to give Fang her lunch. I checked out the tree house, expecting to find her all curled up like I'd left her. No Fang. I looked all around the spots that seemed like they would be a good size for an evil kitten to hide in, but no Fang. I had to find her fast, before one of the other campers or, worse, one of the camp counselors found her! I thought if I gave her a safe place to hang out, she would stay put. I headed back to the tent. Maybe she went there looking for me? That's when I heard Bob, Diablo and Igor inside.

"It was in my backpack! It stole my food!" Bob shouted.

"Is the snake back?" I said as I inched into the

tent, staying very close to the door in case there actually was a real snake in the tent.

"No, more like a squirrel," Diablo said.

"It was bigger than a squirrel," Bob said. "But all I really saw was a gray tail, so I don't know."

Fang. Guess I know why she wasn't in the woods. She was getting her own lunch here.

"What did she take?" I asked.

"She?" Bob said. "Why do you think it's a she?"

"Um, just thinking . . . it's a mother animal getting food for her young?" I made up quickly.

"Well, her young are lucky, then, because she stole my cookie stash. But it mostly just licked out the creamy inside and left the cookies." Bob held up a well-cat-licked cookie to show, and Igor took it, mumbled "urggh" and ate it.

This had Fang written all over it. Eating the creamy filling out of the middle is her favorite thing to do with Oreo cookies. She was totally going to get caught if she kept this up.

Just then, the trumpet sounded again to tell everyone to assemble into their pairs for trap making. I was saved by the off-key *Star Wars* tune.

They were still talking about the cookie theft, though, when we got to the clearing to meet up with our partners.

"Maybe someone brought a pet to camp?" Diablo said. "It could be someone's cat or dog scrambling around for food."

Geeky Girl's voice piped up from next to Bob.

"Around here, your most likely culprit for food theft is a raccoon," she said. "They are clever and can easily get into bags and even cupboards."

"Who asked you?" I said.

"Yeah," Bob added.

"I'm just saying, no one would be stupid enough to bring a cat or dog to camp, would they?" She glared at me. "So it must be a raccoon."

"Maybe it was," I said, grabbing her arm and pulling her away from the guys, "but we gotta get working on our trap. Better get moving." And I stomped off out of earshot of the guys.

"What are you doing?" I said.

"Saving your butt. Again," she said. "But don't thank me."

"I don't need you to save me like *that*," I said. "You could have made it a lot worse. Now I gotta find Fang before she does anything else that could get her caught, and I need her help to do a little sneaky mission too."

"What about our trap?" Geeky Girl said.

"We can plan while we look for her. I have an idea where she might be," I said.

We headed over to the food tent to see if Fang was around, looking for extras for her lunch. If she was hunting for food in our tent, I thought I knew where she would look next.

"There are all kinds of traps we could do," Geeky Girl said. "I made a list of the different general trap categories."

"Of course you did," I muttered. Why did she want to talk about this now? Couldn't she see I was thinking about Fang?

She took out her tablet and read off: "The kinds of traps that catch you in a big net, drop you in a big pit, trap you in a cage, tie you up in ropes, freeze you in a block of ice—"

"Kinda tricky in summer," I interrupted.

"Zombify you, make you fall asleep, trap you in a giant bubble and shoot you into space. Can you think of any more?"

"A trap that bores you to death," I said.

"You got up on the wrong side of the sleeping bag," she mumbled.

"You might not have noticed, but I'm not thinking traps now, OK. I'm thinking pain-in-the-neck disappearing vampire kittens."

Then I spotted Fang. Just inside the kitchen of the mess tent, I could see the gray tail sticking out of a big catering-size can of pork and beans.

At least she's OK. She's going to be found any second and get us both sent home on the Canoe

of Shame, but at least she's OK. There are times I wish I could zombify that kitten.

The cook had his back to us and to Fang. He was clattering around pots and pans, washing them in the sink and singing what I think was a Beyoncé song in Italian. Truly evil. It made enough noise, though, to cover us.

"Can you be lookout for me?" I said to Geeky Girl.

She looked over my shoulder and saw Fang's tail. She rolled her eyes but nodded. "You better be quick. The cook's nearly at the chorus of that song, and I don't want to be here if he starts dancing."

I crept in behind the cook, waiting until the music swelled and the pot banging reached a peak. Then I swooped in and grabbed Fang by the tail with one hand and then immediately covered her mouth to prevent a "MEOW!" with the other hand. I was in and out in a few seconds, and Geeky Girl and I were walking back down to the woods with a muffled, baked-bean-covered Fang stuffed under my jacket.

On the way to the woods, we passed lots of other kids working on their traps.

"Hang on, Igor," I heard the evil Goth girl shout to a mumbling Igor stuck in a net dangling from a tree branch. "I'll just go and get the ax."

"I'm sure the balloon will burst soon from the altitude and the parachute will open," one kid in a white coat said to another as they stared up at the sky. "At least . . . I'm pretty sure."

"Just try not to breathe that much," another kid was saying to a boy in a bubble as she rolled him back toward camp.

"At least no one else's traps seem to be going that well either," I said.

"Maybe we need to come up with a trap that will hold Fang," Geeky Girl said.

Then we saw Dustin and Sanj coming up from the clearing. Without saying a word, both Geeky Girl and I dove behind a tree and hid out of sight.

Sanj and Dustin were both smiling. I didn't like that. Right away I knew their trap was working.

"Excellent work, Dustin. Your knowledge of our animal subjects is invaluable. The birds, squirrels and raccoons you trapped are all behaving within required parameters. The groundwork for our master trap is complete. We just need our final subject," Sanj said.

"Oh, we'll get him," Dustin said. "You just need to make sure the device is powered up and ready to use."

"Of course," Sanj said. He stopped just by the tree we were hidden behind and sniffed the air. "Do you smell beans?"

15

Dustin took a deep sniff.

"No," he said, "but now I'm hungry. Let's head back so we're early for dinner. Oh, and we must wash our hands, as we've been in contact with the animals."

"You are so right," Sanj said. "One can't be too careful about germs." And they walked on back toward camp.

One thing about not working with Sanj was him not making me clean up stuff and telling me I was messy all the time. I looked down at my baked-bean-, dirt- and kitten-fur-covered hands, then wiped them on my shirt. "So their plan is something to do with trapping birds and animals, huh?" Geeky Girl said, standing up.

I stood up too and took Fang out of my jacket. She had completely clawed up the lining already and had smeared beans everywhere too. "You nearly gave us away again, kitten," I said as I put her on the ground. She rolled over on the grass and licked the last of the beans off her fur.

I heard a fluttering overhead and then saw the green-and-yellow feathers come into view. Boris swooped down and landed on Geeky Girl's shoulder. And for a split second I was jealous. I

was jealous of her low-maintenance pet who didn't get itself into trouble, didn't swipe food or scratch things, and didn't nearly get caught and get us thrown out of camp.

Then Fang pounced, and I caught myself thinking proudly, "Yeah, that's my little evil kitten."

So sue me. I *am* mostly evil.

Fang sprung up to Geeky Girl's shoulder and knocked that smug little budgie right off. They both tumbled to the ground and rolled apart. Fang and Boris circled each other, beak, teeth and claws at the ready.

Geeky Girl scrambled on the ground, trying to catch Boris, and I stood behind Fang, trying to block her getting at the bird.

"I knew we should have trapped that kitten. We have to stop them fighting," she said.

"The only way to stop Fang trying to get Boris is if she's already got him," I said.

Then I had one another evil lightbulb moment. And this one had nothing to do with ketchup. "Or she thinks that she's already got him!" I mumbled.

"What?" Geeky Girl asked.

"That's our trap. A kinda virtual-trap thing that makes the trappee think they've already been trapped!" I said.

Her face went blank for a sec, like she was rebooting, and after a pause she shouted, "That's genius. That's totally evil genius."

She jumped up and down on the spot so much that both Fang and Boris scampered out of the way so they wouldn't get bounced on by mistake. Boris cooed and flapped back up to her shoulder, while Fang slunk over and curled around my feet.

"Like a virtual game?" I said. "The person would see a trap that wasn't there. Can we do that?"

"I brought some 3-D goggles. We could modify them and upload a program with the virtual trap inside." Geeky Girl was in full planning mode now.

"Yeah, but we would have to trick the person who you want to trap into wearing the goggles," I said, my own evil-plan brain switching into action mode.

"We can work on that," she said. "But I think this could be the trap that wins!"

"It totally beats some lame animal trap like Sanj and Dustin have," I said. "They are using something out of our notebook too. I know it! I gotta get that notebook back, Fang. Do you think you can sneak it out of Sanj's jacket pocket without getting caught?"

Fang purred a totally confident purr.

"Then we can make our amazing virtual trap and have the notebook so they can't steal any more of my genius ideas. Result!" I said.

I started to raise a hand to fist-bump Geeky Girl, but then pulled back. "Cool, umm, we can get all the tech stuff together tonight and work on it tomorrow. We better head back to camp. I have to hide Fang again before the guys get back to the tent. And there might even be time to do a little notebook hunting, hey, Fang?"

Geeky Girl looked at her watch. "You might not have time," she said. "Phillipe Fortescue is doing his talk on evil disguises before dinner, remember?"

The Darth Vader trumpet sounded again.

"See. You'll have to take Fang with you to the talk."

Boris flapped off Geeky Girl's shoulder and up into the branches of the trees.

"Man, that's not fair. Boris can just blend in 'cause he's a bird," I said.

"You can't disguise the fact that Fang is a kitten, and kittens aren't supposed to be at camp," she said. Then she stopped and added, "Or maybe you can?"

16

"Maybe you can what?" I said to Geeky Girl.

"Disguise Fang." She smiled. "That's what we're going to be learning. How to disguise yourself to blend in. So what could we make Fang look like to blend in with her surroundings?"

We quickly tried covering Fang in leaves to look like a bush, but she rustled and shook everything off in seconds. We started to try again, but Fang jumped away from us, brushing against some leftover charcoal on the ground from last night's campfire. It left a blackish streak on her fur.

"That's it!" I said, an idea forming. "She needs makeup. Charcoal makeup."

I pulled Fang onto my lap and grabbed the piece of charcoal. "Close your eyes, kitten," I said, and drew a blackish Zorro mask around her eyes and lines around her ears. I blackened her paws and drew rings around her tail. She was no longer a simple gray kitten; she was a little, striped, masked raccoon.

"Now if anyone spots her, they won't think it's weird that a raccoon is hanging around camp. And if she gets into our tent, then you've already told the guys how clever raccoons are, so they'll buy that too." I paused. "That was kinda a smart thing to say."

"Thanks. You know something that I never thought I would say about Fang? She does look kinda cute like that." Geeky Girl smiled.

Fang hissed at her, and jumped down from my lap, making Geeky Girl step back.

"What do you say, kitten? Want to hide out as a raccoon for a while?"

Fang didn't look impressed.

"Actually, I hate to attribute a negative attitude to any animal, but raccoons are pretty evil," Geeky Girl said, and shrugged her shoulders.

"She's right, kitten." I stroked Fang's ear, careful not to rub off the charcoal. "They swipe stuff; they're sneaky; they break into things and mess up stuff. They are way more evil than kittens."

Fang swiped at my fingers. I got them out of the way just in time.

"Not you, of course, but more evil than most kittens," I said. "It might be fun to pretend to be an evil raccoon for a while, right? Plus, if Sanj or Dustin spots you when you're notebook-hunting, then they can only blame the raccoon. Mwhaaa-haa-haa-haa."

I scooped her up and tucked her inside my jacket again and gave her some of my burger from lunch to keep her quiet.

Geeky Girl and I headed back toward camp. We stopped by Sanj and Dustin's tent, and I let Fang jump out of my jacket. "OK, Fang, let's see if you can get in raccoon character and swipe my notebook back while we go to the disguise talk. Remember, stay out of sight and don't get into any trouble."

Fang meowed at me in a way that I swear in Cat meant, "You're telling *me* to stay outta trouble?!"

When we got back, I spotted the guys so quickly, I ditched Geeky Girl and headed off to sit with them.

"Yeah, OK, I'll just work on all that stuff for the genius idea for our trap, then, shall I?" she shouted after me as I walked off.

"Yeah, good," I said. "We can work on it tomorrow. I'm with my evil posse now, OK."

"Your evil posse? Please," she mumbled.

Phillipe's talk about disguises was mega boring until he got to the part where we each had to learn how to camouflage ourselves as an object around camp.

Bob wanted to be a basketball hoop. Fair enough. He's pretty tall.

Diablo wanted to be a tree, but a tree cut into a totem pole design. Way too much work, if you ask me.

And Igor wanted to be a sleeping bag. He made a really good sleeping bag, actually. People kept sitting on him 'cause he just looked so comfortable, you know. Phillipe showed us how to use makeup and props to transform ourselves. He had this whole huge bag of stuff to camouflage us all.

I had no idea what I wanted to be.

Phillipe was going to get to me any second. He already was turning Dustin into a large red maple leaf. I was next.

At that point, I heard a scratching sound and saw a raccoon tail disappear under a log.

17

Now was this an actual raccoon or Fang in disguise?

Then I heard Igor shouting, "URGGGHHHH!" from over by the log.

I ran over and saw the raccoon standing on top of the still-very-comfortable-looking sleeping bag, aka Igor, kneading it with her claws, like cats do when they want to sit somewhere. This was definitely my evil kitten. Fang was just curling up to fall asleep when the bag wriggled and shook her off. Igor had flicked his leg, which sent her flying into the nearest tree.

Fortunately, Fang has quick reflexes and turned instantly so she hit the tree trunk claws-first and stuck.

Unfortunately, that tree trunk was actually Diablo's tree before the totem pole makeup went on.

"ARRRRRRGGGGHHHHH!" he screamed. "Get this loco raccoon off me!"

Sanj was standing right next to him but stepped

back behind some other kids. "No, that thing might have rabies!"

Dustin started to pull out something from under his jacket. I couldn't see what it was, though, in all the commotion. I heard Sanj whisper, "We can't. It will give away the whole plan. Put it away."

"Get the rabid raccoon off me," Diablo repeated. Fang was scared now, and when she's scared, she digs in more with her claws. She wasn't going anywhere if she could help it, but I had to get her out of there before someone spotted that she wasn't a loco raccoon, after all. Besides there was no way any of these people were getting their hands on my little vampire kitten!

Phillipe stepped through the kids and pushed them out of the way.

"Just shoo it away and get on with the practice," he said. "You can't let this kind of thing blow your cover. I once had a pigeon nest in my hair for three days while I was disguised as a telephone pole to intercept communications. Did I blow my cover? Even when the phone company came out to do repairs? No. So neither should you!"

He was almost at Fang now. If he got closer, he might notice that she wasn't actually a raccoon. I wasn't sure, but I think a master of disguise could figure out our trick.

"I got it, sir!" I said, and ran past him. I scooped
Fang off the tree (I think taking part of Diablo's
T-shirt with me) and kept running, while holding
her out in front of me well away from any swinging
claws.

"I'm gonna dump it far into the woods, sir!" I
shouted back.

"Good, now that the Snake Boy has taken care
of the wild creature, we can get back to actually
learning something," Phillipe said. "Honestly,
how evil can you be if you are scared of a little
raccoon?" he mumbled.

Then I could just about hear him saying, "You,
the girl standing on your own. I think you would
make a very lifelike shrub."

I kept running until we were well out of sight.
Fang had given up swiping a few trees back. When
I got to the tree house again, I sat on a rock and let
her down on the ground.

"Once again, Fang, you nearly got caught!" I said.

She glared at me like she was angry, but then curled around my ankles and head-butted me until I petted her. Black soot from the charcoal came off on my hand.

I pulled out a spare piece that I had pocketed and touched up the black rings on her fur. "We have to keep you looking like a raccoon, Fang."

She purred and sat up so I could reach her paws and face. "There. Now let's head back and get some dinner. I guess they won't think it's odd if a raccoon swipes something from my plate." I paused. "Someone else's plate would be better if you can, though."

As we walked back toward camp, through the forest, Fang suddenly hunched down into full-attack cat mode. Her fur stood on end and her eyes widened. She saw something and was stalking it.

18

I wasn't sure if she was about to attack a hot dog that some camper had dropped after lunch or if she had stumbled onto somebody's evil trap.

She crept closer and closer to a bush by the clearing.

Then I saw it. A few feathers from a green wing were sticking out of the bush. Fang leaned back and pawed the ground in front of her, ready to pounce. Then I heard "Don't even think about it, Fang!" from inside the bush.

"Geeky Girl?" I asked, shaking the shrub to see if she was in there.

"It's my disguise." She popped her head up from between some branches, and Boris flew off a safe distance away onto a tree branch overhead. "Philippe decided I would make a good shrub." She started pulling off her camouflage of branches. "Wait, do you hear something?"

I would recognize that evil wheeze anywhere.

"It's Sanj. And probably Dustin too." I looked around. "Quick, hide."

She popped back into the bush while I picked up some branches from the shrub disguise that she had thrown onto the ground. I crouched and covered myself with the branches. I couldn't see where Fang had gone. She was still marked up as a raccoon, but I didn't like her out there with Sanj and Dustin. She was already in a pouncing mood. What if she grabbed the notebook now, or what if she just jumped them 'cause she was bored?

"We are totally gonna win that Evil Emperor of the Week for this trap," Dustin said.

"I have no doubt in your trapping expertise on the matter," Sanj said. "And my invention will ensure that our final subject complies with the plan."

His invention? I thought. Then I saw it. Sanj took the Nicifying Helpful Minion Ray out from under his jacket and patted it. They had rebuilt it, sure, but it was definitely our design. I liked that floppy-haired kid even less now. He not only stole my evil pal, he stole my evil plans as well.

"Hey, don't point that thing at me," Dustin said, pushing the barrel of the ray gun back toward the ground.

"Sorry," Sanj said. "Let's find our big friend." They walked off farther into the woods.

Geeky Girl and I both dropped our branches and stepped out from the bush when they had gone.

"Was that the Nicifying Helpful Minion Ray?" Geeky Girl asked.

"Yup," I said, staring after them.

"The same one that turned you nice and . . . ," she added.

"Let's not talk about that," I said. "I don't ever talk about that." I shuddered at the thought of my day of making tea, playing pat-a-cake with Sami and doing absolutely nothing at all that was even remotely evil while I was under the control of the Nicifying Helpful Minion Ray. It was the saddest day of my young life. Except for the fact that it was also the day I met Fang.

"They must have used the ray on some animals, or are planning to," I said. "Remember, they were trapping them before."

"Unless they were just testing it on animals . . . ? It sounds like they are going to use it on a person," Geeky Girl said.

"Yeah, they did say 'our big friend,'" I said. "There's no way they are getting me with that gun again."

"Maybe they mean Igor? He's probably the biggest kid here," she said.

I smiled thinking of Igor sitting, making cups of tea. Then I snapped out of it.

"He's in my evil tent posse," I said. "I have to warn him if Sanj and Dustin are up to something. We don't know anything for sure, though, so I'll let him know to stay away from Sanj and Dustin just in case."

"OK, you go talk to Igor, and I'll finish the modifications to the 3-D goggles," Geeky Girl said.

"Come on," I said, and we started to walk back to the camp. "Um, do you want to go in first so it doesn't look like we are, you know, hanging out or anything? I got the posse to think of."

"Of course you do." Geeky Girl shook her head and strode off down the trail back to camp with Boris fluttering behind her.

"Girls just don't get it, do they?" I mumbled to Fang as I started to scoop her up to take her back to camp. She meowed and swiped me. I honestly think that one was a swipe for femalekind.

19

When we got back, I put Fang down behind some logs by the campfire clearing.

"OK, my little evil cat burglar, can you go and find that Evil Plans Notebook in Sanj's tent while they're at dinner?" She purred and slunk off toward the tents.

It was going to be soooo good when I got that notebook back.

In the meantime I had to warn Igor. I found him dozing as everyone was lining up to get their food for dinner. He was still in disguise as a sleeping bag and still looked really comfortable. I got sleepy just looking at him. I shoved away another camp kid who was about to sit on him and crouched down on the ground.

"Hey, Igor," I said, and shook what I thought was his shoulder, but actually was a leg. "Wake up, man, or you'll miss dinner."

"Urgh," he said, and nodded.

"Um, and another thing, um, you might want to stay away from Sanj and Dustin for the next day, until the contest is over. I just heard something. I'm not sure or anything, but I don't trust them," I added.

"Urgh, urgh," Igor said, and got up.

We walked to dinner together, and I lined up behind him with my tray. Soon Diablo and Bob fell in behind us.

"Hey, Mark. We're gonna put the final touches on our trap tonight," Bob said.

"Yeah, you want to help us?" Diablo said. "We're meeting down by the edge of the woods after dinner."

"Sure," I said. "Our trap is totally under control, so I can help with yours too. No sweat." Result. Mark the Snake-in-ator is still in demand. I can win with my trap, but still help my evil posse come in second.

I saw Sanj and Dustin get in line to get their dinner.

"How's your little project with Geeky Girl going?" Sanj sneered as he scooped up the evil casserole on offer.

"It's totally going to beat any lame trap that you're doing," I said. "I'm so far along on our trap that I'm even taking time to help out Bob and Diablo with theirs. That's how good my trap is," I said. "And Igor here, his trap is way better too. . . . It's . . . It's . . ." I turned to Igor. "What is your trap, anyway?"

Igor mimed a giant net, then mimed the giant net ripping.

"OK. Igor's is broken, but it was a way better trap than yours anyway. So there," I said.

Igor nodded. "Urgh." I noticed he stepped back a little from Sanj and Dustin.

"You'll see tomorrow evening." Sanj smiled. "All will be revealed." Then he did his evil wheeze and headed off to sit with Dustin.

"That guy should see a doctor about that wheeze," Bob said.

After dinner, I went over to the log to give Fang some casserole, but she wasn't there. So I headed back to the tree house to check on her. As I approached, I could hear breathing coming from inside the hut. I pulled myself up on a low branch so I could peek over the edge. I could just make out a gray tail sticking out from under my sweatshirt. And what looked like the corner of my Evil Plans Notebook under the tail. Result! Fang the super stealer had gotten it. I wanted to grab it right away, but she looked cute when she was asleep. Not that I would ever tell her that or admit it to anyone here. Still, I guess she'd had a long day. She might as well sleep. She was only missing mystery evil casserole anyway for dinner. I'd bring her double sausage in the morning and pocket that evil notebook too. I let myself have a little "Mwhaa-haa-haa" whisper as I headed up to the edge of the woods. It was just starting to get dark when I got there. Bob and Diablo were covering up a place on the ground with branches.

"Oh, so it's the old cover-up-a-hole-with-branches-and-the-person-falls-in kind of trap?" I said. "Yeah, I'm not gonna fall for that one." I walked carefully around the branches.

Suddenly, the ground beneath my feet gave way and I tumbled into the darkness of their pit trap.

"Urmph!" I spluttered as I fell backward onto my butt.

I could hear laughing up at the top of the pit, and then I could see Diablo's and Bob's faces looking over the side down at me. "You should have seen your face when you fell, man!" Diablo laughed.

"That was classic," Bob said in between heaving laughs.

"OK, you got me," I said. "That's a good fake-out on the classic pit trap."

"Oh, that isn't the only catch with this trap," Bob said.

"We asked you to help out with this 'cause we knew you wouldn't be freaked out by the next bit," Diablo said. "Snake-in-ator."

Then I heard the hissing. In the dark, behind me in the hole. I couldn't see anything, but I could hear it. "Hhhhiiissssssss."

20

"Fang . . . ?" I whispered, hoping that somehow it was my evil little kitten and not some big bitey snake that was really unhappy about being put down in a pit with people nearly falling on him.

Then I saw the eyes. A glow of two yellow slits in the darkness.

"What is that? Guys, come on. Let me up now," I said, keeping my cool—barely.

"Dude, it's just another snake," Diablo shouted down. "You totally took care of the one in the tent, no problem."

"Yeah, we want to see how long it will take you to fight off the snake and escape the trap so we can see how well it works before tomorrow," Bob said. "No big deal. It's just a snake, right?"

"Yeah, just a snake," I said, backing away from the glowing eyes in front of me. I tried to reach up and grab for a root or a branch or something. "It's too easy, guys. Ya know? Might as well pull me up now, right?"

"Come on, Mark, we need to know how long it takes you to fight the snake," Bob said.

"Hey, you know, maybe we should have put two snakes in there," Diablo started to say, just as the snake flicked its tongue out toward me and stretched its mouth open wide.

"OK, your trap wins. Just let me up now. The snake is for real!" I hollered up. I had to get out of there. I tried to climb up the dirt walls of the pit, but it was too slippery, and I kept sliding down. My palms were sweating so much that the dirt was forming into sweaty mud cakes on my hands as I clawed at the walls.

I landed with another thud in a puddle at the bottom of the pit, splashing into the darkness where the eyes lurked. I don't think the snake liked being splashed. It slithered out and circled me.

"Get me out, guys! This isn't funny!" I shouted, but they just laughed.

Then there was another splash and something joined me in the pit.

Fear gripped my body as my eyes adjusted to the dark. Was it another snake? But then I saw two more eyes. These ones were green and bright with a distinctly evil flash in them. Fang!

I could hear Bob say, "The raccoon just jumped straight in. Weird."

Fang darted through the puddle and jumped straight at the snake.

"Be careful, Fang!" I shouted to her.

"Are you talking to the raccoon?" Diablo shouted. Then I heard, "I think maybe he knocked his head when he fell in."

Fang and the snake were rolling around in
the mud. I could hear her hiss and meow, and the
snake hissed right back.

"That doesn't sound like a raccoon. That
sounds like a cat," Diablo said.

"And that hiss sounds like a cat's hiss. That was
the hiss from the tent the other night," Bob said. "It
wasn't a snake at all. It was a cat in the tent!"

I should have been worried that they had just
uncovered my whole snake fake-out plan, but I was
too worried about Fang being swallowed whole by
an angry viper.

"Fang, watch out!" I shouted as the snake tried
to bite her tail.

She was fast, though, as she dashed under and

around the coils of the snake. Maybe she was
trying to tire it out. Maybe she was waiting to get
a good bite in somewhere. I don't know what went
on inside that evil-kitten head, but whatever she
was doing, she seemed like she had a plan. That is,
right up until the snake started to squeeze.

I could see that it had wrapped itself around her
and gotten her tail in its coils. Something snapped
in me, and I reached out to pull at the wriggling
snake, to try to pull Fang free. It was too strong,
though. The snake turned its head toward me
and snapped just as I pulled my arm back. In that
moment, Fang had rolled herself and the snake
into the puddle. With a squelch of muddy fur she
managed to slide her tail out of the slippery coils.

She turned on the snake, and with a fierce kitten meow she jumped behind it, then to its left, its right, under and over she ran. The snake followed the kitten's movements, trying to grab her tail with its open mouth. She was always one inch ahead of the jaws. Just as the snake twisted to follow her and attack, it suddenly stopped.

21

I stared at the snake as it strained and pulled, but it was stuck. Fang leaped far out of reach of the snake, looked on and purred a massively smug purr. She had managed to get the snake to tie itself up in knots.

It rolled around trying to undo itself.

I think I breathed for the first time since Fang had pounced on that snake. She was OK.

Fang jumped up into my arms. She was soaked through from the puddle water and all the charcoal markings had washed off. She looked like her normal gray kitteny self. For a second I forgot that my friends were about to see that I was a fake, that my whole time at camp was probably over and that I would never get to wear that stupid nonexistent

emperor crown. I just stroked her head and took
another breath.

Bob and Diablo looked over the side and shone
a flashlight in my face. "It's a kitten," Bob said. "You
saved us from a hissing kitten the other night?!"

"Yeah, some Snake-in-ator, man," Diablo said.

Then I heard Geeky Girl's voice as a rope
was dropped down into the hole and fell on my
shoulder. "Grab it and climb up!" she shouted.

Fang climbed into my pocket, and I heaved us
up the side of the pit by the rope, which Geeky
Girl had tied to a nearby tree. When I got to the
top, I pulled myself over the side.

"Wait till the rest of the campers hear that Mark the Snake-in-ator had to be rescued by a tiny kitten!" Bob laughed.

"I didn't need to be rescued. I was just kidding with you guys. I nearly had that snake just where I wanted him, if that stupid kitten hadn't gotten in the way...!"

I knew it as soon as I said it. You know how sometimes you can almost see the words leaving your mouth and you wish that you could catch them as they fly out. It was like that.

It was like those words were flying out and all hitting Fang in the face as I said them.

She jumped out of my pocket and bolted for the woods.

The boys just laughed again.

"I think you lost your kitten now, dude," Bob said. Then he said something else, and Geeky Girl said something to them too, but I stopped listening. I took off after Fang. "Wait, Fang!" I shouted into the darkness of the woods. "I didn't mean it. Wait!"

I headed to the tree house first and was so relieved when I heard the breathing inside and saw the gray tail sticking out of my sweatshirt like before. But hang on. This tail had definite raccoon markings on it, and the charcoal markings on Fang's tail had been all washed off in the puddle. This wasn't Fang. I shook the edge of my sweatshirt, and an actual, non-charcoaled raccoon face peered out from under it.

"Arrrrraaaahhhh!" I screamed.

"RRReeeeaaaaol," it screeched, and scratched its claws on my sweatshirt and did what raccoons apparently do when you scare them in the middle of a nap. It peed all over the tree house. Then it scrambled past me, out of the tree house and back into the woods.

I looked at my shredded raccoon-pee-soaked sweatshirt and my shredded raccoon-pee-soaked Evil Plans Notebook. Today couldn't get any worse. But it could. Fang was still missing and she still hated me.

I had to find her. I looked everywhere I could think of for her. In the woods, then in the kitchen tent, by the campfire area, by the pier, by where Geeky Girl had been a shrub this afternoon. But Fang wasn't anywhere. She wouldn't have gone back to the tent, and now neither could I. By breakfast, every kid in camp was going to know that I had made up the whole snake-fighting thing and that I was a fake.

Worse, they probably figured out that Fang was my pet, and I would be thrown out before I had a chance to win the contest or stop Sanj. But worst of all—Fang hated me.

I went to the base of the tree house in case she came back that way, wrapped my Evil Scientist coat around me and tried to get some sleep.

22

The next day, I was woken up by the same evil Darth Vader music, but this time it was played on a piccolo. It's pretty hard to make anything sound evil on a piccolo, really.

I opened my eyes, and Geeky Girl was standing next to the tree. She held out a cold bacon sandwich.

"I picked it up at breakfast," she said. I took it and started to sit up.

"Igor said you didn't go back to the tent last night," she added.

"Igor actually said that?" I asked.

"Well, not exactly. But he urghed and pointed, and I got what he meant."

"Yeah, well, I didn't want to be laughed at all night," I said. "Besides, I had to look for Fang."

"Did you find her?" Geeky Girl asked.

"No," I said, "she's gone."

"I can't find Boris this morning either. I'm worried," she added.

"What's the point?" I mumbled as I bit into the bacon sandwich. "Mmmfhng mand mai mare maonna meacet kicmmeout manyllmay."

"What?" Geeky Girl was staring at me as I chewed and talked.

"I said, Fang and I are going to get kicked out anyway—not that Fang will ever want to see me again—so what's the point? Bob and Diablo will tell the camp counselors that I have a kitten at camp and we'll be sent home."

"They don't know Fang is your kitten," Geeky

Girl said. "I told them last night after you ran off that people had spotted this kitten roaming around the camp, but it didn't belong to anyone. It must be a stray."

"So they won't tell everyone about how scared I was of the snake and how Fang rescued me either?" I asked hopefully.

"Oh, no, they already told everyone that. Like everyone." She grimaced. "I think they are calling you Mark the Fake-in-ator now."

I slumped back against the side of the tree house. "I'm ruined."

"Hey, why did you make up that story about Fang being a stray?" I said.

Geeky Girl pushed back her hair from her face. "You know. If they find one pet, they'll look out for more. I'm protecting Boris . . . ," she started to say.

"I get that you want to protect your pet, but if it was to be nice to me, then I don't get it," I said. Then I breathed in and looked at the dirt, because ya know, I'm mostly evil and hate ever saying nice stuff. "I was beyond evil to you, like, most of the time, but I'm sorry about saying whatever to Sanj at the campfire, and I'm sorry I ditched you too. Even if they find out about Fang, I promise I won't snitch on Boris."

"Overt Niceness will not be tolerated." She smiled at me. "Rule Number 2 of the Evil Camp Code . . . You're gonna get kicked out for that now."

"Never call me nice," I said.

"OK, you're back to normal," she added. "Look, they won't find out about Boris or Fang," she said. "And we can still win this contest. Then you can actually say you won this for real and not because you faked it," she said. "I have the 3-D goggles all programmed. I've even sewed the goggles into one of my beanies so, you know, whoever wears it will still look cool. We just need to set the trap. But first, we have to find Fang and Boris."

As we headed back to Geeky Girl's tent to get all the equipment, an announcement blasted out of the speakers.

"Attention, campers. Zhis is zee last morning to work on your traps. The remaining teams vill show zeir projects zis afternoon to the group by the campfire grounds."

"What does he mean, remaining teams?" I asked.

"To update you on zee missing teams. We have picked up the SOS from zee submarine trap made by Meagan and Sven. We have tracked them down to a point off the coast and are sending out a ship to intercept zem. The team with the balloon has been spotted just over zee next mountain range, so we're hoping to bring zhem down later zhis morning.

"Zee exploding bubble in the trumpet trap went badly wrong, but we are hoping to free both the team members and the trumpet by tomorrow," Trevor continued.

"Ah, that explains the piccolo this morning,"
Geeky Girl and I both said at the same time.

"Good luck—or should I say 'evil luck'?—
with your traps, and may the most evil team win.
Mwhaa-haa-haaa-haaa." The announcement ended.

Igor stomped over to us and grunted.

"Hi, Igor," I said. "So you're still talking to me
even though I'm now a Fake-in-ator?"

"Urgh," Igor said, and nodded.

"Hey, Igor," Geeky Girl said. "Did you happen
to see a small green budgie and a little gray kitten
anywhere around this morning?"

"Not that they have anything to do with us or
anything, but we were just wondering," I added.

Igor stared at us with a look that said "What?"
and then shook his head.

"Urgh, Urgh Urgh!" he added, though, and
started pointing toward the woods.

"You saw something else this morning?" Geeky
Girl asked.

Igor acted out a longish mime that involved
tossing back his hair like he was in a shampoo

commercial and wheezing a very poor "Mwh-urgh-Mwh-urgh-Mwh-urgh" laugh.

"You spotted Sanj and Dustin this morning heading down to the woods?" I said.

"Urgh." Igor nodded. Then he made a shape with his fingers like he was holding a pretend ray gun. "Urgh-zap, urgh-zap."

23

"It's a Nicifying Helpful Minion Ray," I explained to Igor, but I could tell that didn't really mean anything to him. "It's part of their trap. That was the thing I thought they might want to use on you, Igor. They mentioned 'trying it on the big guy,' so you know, I thought of you."

Igor slapped me on the back. I think it was supposed to be friendly, but it took me a minute to breathe again after.

"Y-yeah." I coughed. "No problem, man. But I guess it wasn't you they were after, or they would have used it on you then."

"You don't have an overwhelming urge to smile and drink tea, do you?" Geeky Girl asked. "Because that would mean you were shot with the ray, but didn't realize it."

I interrupted. "I don't think Igor smiles easily, and if he did, it would be for totally evil reasons, right, Igor?"

Igor nodded.

"Look, Sanj and Dustin must have adapted the ray gun to do something else, or they would have used it on us too. It works on animals and makes them do what you say, so maybe they are using it on wild animals this time, instead of pets," Geeky Girl suggested.

"They were setting traps the other day. They could have an army of animals by now," I said.

"Urgh!" Igor said, and pointed to the woods again.

"Yeah, and that's where the army is, then," I said. "Let's go and see what kind of trap they have in mind."

Kids started coming out of their tents and heading off in different directions to work on their projects. I could hear some laughing and some mumbles of "Fake-in-ator" too.

"Igor is hanging with the Fake-in-ator, and that totally unevil-looking chick," the Goth girl that was teamed up with Igor shouted. "He was only good for getting caught in our own trap, anyway. Evil loser." She sneered and walked off with some of the other kids.

"Hey, Igor, you know, you can, like, push me over or something if you want to make it look like you're not with us," I said, bracing myself for his big arms to shove me. "Just don't do it too hard, ya know, big guy."

Igor shook his head and stomped off toward the woods. Great, so I was the loser of camp now, and everyone who went near me, even big old evil Igor, was labeled a loser too. I was not only ruined, I was toxic to anyone else. I thought it couldn't get any worse, but as Geeky Girl and I started to follow Igor, we were intercepted by Kirsty Katastrophe and Phillipe Fortescue walking back to the counselors' tents.

"So Snake Kid is really Fake Kid," Kirsty drawled. "I should've known. Rule One of faking an evil win is 'Don't get caught!'" Then she turned and called out to the other campers walking by, "Fake-in-ator here has given me an idea for a new evil mantra: Every day and every way you're getting more and more pathetic." Then as the other kids all laughed, she held up her hand, which was holding an evil pom-pom at the time, right in front of my face.

"But I didn't mean . . . ," I started.

"Talk to the pom-pom, because the face isn't listening," she said, and strode off.

"I hope that your trap isn't as embarrassing as your snake stunt, or you'll be on the next canoe out of camp," Phillipe added. "Tsk tsk. And you made a passable shrub as well," he mumbled to Geeky Girl.

OK, so I have gone from hero to zero in less than twelve hours. Kirsty thinks I'm a loser. Phillipe thinks I'm a loser. Trevor probably couldn't even be bothered to think about what I am, because I'm such a loser. I could still get kicked out for my smuggled vampire kitten at any time. If I could find her, that is! Even if I do find her, Fang will never speak to me again. Everyone is laughing at me except a totally not-evil computer-nerd girl and a big mostly evil thug, and now he's probably not talking to me either. Not that there's much talking with Igor, but not grunting at you in Igor speak is just as bad.

I almost wished I was back in that hole with the snake.

By the time Geeky Girl and I got to the edge of
the woods, there was no sign of Igor, Fang or Boris.

Then we heard a whistle coming from deeper
in the woods, and I spotted a green flash of feathers
fly past in the trees overhead.

"Boris?" Geeky girl said.

24

"Maybe Boris has seen Fang?" I said to Geeky Girl.

We followed the sound of the whistle, and it led us to a clearing where there were already dozens of squirrels, raccoons and different birds and animals all standing still. Like they were waiting for something. It was spooky, but also familiar. I don't remember everything from being shot with the Nicifying Helpful Minion Ray, but I do remember that stare. These animals had that same eerie stare. I got a shiver down my back.

"Boris!" Geeky Girl whispered up to a branch in a tree as she crept around behind it. Boris just sat there, though. He always fluttered down to sit on her shoulder (or creepily kind of hover over it), but this time he just ignored her. She stood there by the side of the tree while I moved into the clearing. If Boris was here, then maybe . . .

I looked around, and there among all the other animals on the ground I spotted a furry gray tail. "Fang?" I couldn't hold back. I ran up to her into the circle of animals. "Fang? Are you OK?" I said as I approached. She hadn't even flinched. Not a flick of her tail, not a swipe of her paw. It was weird.

Suddenly, Sanj and Dustin strode out from behind a tree and stepped into the group of animals.

"Consider this payback for stealing back the Evil Plans Notebook from my tent last night. There was gray fur on my pillow when I got back. Dead giveaway."

"I don't have the Evil Plans Notebook anymore. It got . . . well, it actually got shredded and peed on by a raccoon. But the point is, I don't have it either, so now neither of us can use the stuff we came up with, and that kind of makes it even, right? Um . . . so you can just let the pets go and get on with whatever weird animal army thing you've got going on here," I said.

"I don't think so." Sanj smiled a truly evil smile. "I thought I was happy when I got to use the ray gun on the annoying nasty kitten and the ridiculous bird, but now this is even better."

"Sanj," I said, "you need to let the pets go, or I will . . . I will . . ." I raised my fists.

"Ah, ah, ah," Dustin tutted. "No unauthorized violence at Evil Scientist Summer Camp."

"I'll unauthorize you . . . ," I started to say, but stopped myself. "Look, you don't need Fang and

Boris for your trap to work, right? Whatever wacko trap you have going on, you must have had it all planned with the squirrels and raccoons and stuff, so maybe you can just let the pets go. And you can get on with finishing your trap, and we can get on with ours."

"We?" Dustin said.

I looked around, about to say, "Yeah, Geeky Girl and me," when I noticed that she was nowhere to be seen. She must have hidden when she saw Sanj and Dustin come out.

"I mean . . . ummm . . . we . . . ummm . . . me and the pets . . . yeah," I covered. "You don't need them, so just let them go."

"Of course we don't NEED them," Sanj said, "but it's so much more fun with them in the mix." He smiled evilly. "Especially since you are now caught in the trap yourself."

"I'm not caught in anything," I said. "Like I'm so scared of a bunch of birds and squirrels, anyway."

Then Dustin blew the whistle again and dozens more animals poured into the clearing.

They formed a circle around me, and then started piling up into a kind of animal wall. It was weird. In minutes, the wall was taller than me. The shiver down my back turned into a full-on shudder as it climbed all the way back up my spine again. How many animals had they gotten in their trap? There must have been hundreds.

All I could see was this pile of fur and feathers. Fang was up and to my left, on top of a couple of raccoons and a ferret and with a crow perched on her back. I tried to reach out to stroke her, to get her to snap out of things. She hissed and swiped, but just stared ahead. She had no idea who I was or even if I was there.

"If you hurt Fang with this stupid trap . . ."
I could barely get the words out between my
clenched teeth.

"Please do be quiet, Mark. It's hard enough to
concentrate on things with all this squawking and
hissing, but now I have to measure the radius of
our trap so we can realign the perimeter reading."

"What?" I shouted back.

"Just *shhhh*!" Sanj yelled. "Dustin, can you
please put down the Nicifying Helpful Minion Ray
and help me pace out the distance with this tape?"

I craned my neck to see through a hole in
the wall of animals. There was a small gap. Just
between the tail of a big gray squirrel and the
ears of a pretty rough-looking rabbit, I could see
Dustin leaning the ray gun against a tree. Then I
saw a hand very slowly and quietly reach out and
grab the ray gun.

25

Geeky Girl. Yes! Result! She got the gun!

"Right, Sanj, it's seven meters," Dustin said. "So I guess it's time to try out the big guy."

"You won't find Igor around here to zap him with the ray," I shouted.

"Who says we're talking about Igor?" Sanj laughed a particularly wheezy evil laugh.

"Seriously, you should see a doctor about that, dude," Dustin said. Then he blew the whistle in a different way.

Geeky Girl peeked her head out from behind the tree and tried to mouth a message to me. I think she might have been mouthing, "I've switched the polarity on the gun so that it reverses things. I'm going to try to isolate Fang and Boris in the beam, and hopefully that will free them from the hypnotic ray." Or she may have said something about polar bears having a nice day.

I heard a muffled zappy noise and a rustling of feathers and saw Boris fly out of his perch between two dazed-looking blue jays.

Sanj and Dustin still seemed distracted, looking out into the woods for whatever they were waiting for.

Then another zap and Fang shook her head. She hissed at the crow and ferret and shook herself free. She looked over at me for a second, and she looked like she was going to run to me but changed her mind. She leaped out of the circle and ran toward the tree that Geeky Girl still hid behind, obviously still mad at me for last night. It was like a kick in the stomach. Even when faced with a wall of creepy-stare animals, she would rather run away from me than come to me.

"Did you hear something?" Dustin said, and turned around.

"Maybe it's the big guy?" Sanj suggested.

So if "the big guy" isn't Igor, then who is this secret weapon in their evil trap plan?

Did they hypno one of the counselors or trap a park ranger or something?

There was a rustling in the trees heading for the clearing.

"Sanj, did you pick up the Nicifying Helpful Minion Ray?" Dustin asked. "Because I swear I leaned it against that tree."

Geeky Girl peeked out and mouthed me another message. I think this one said, "I'm trying to reset the ray gun so it can unhypnotize all the animals at once. That should free you."

Then the rustling got louder and was followed

by some serious stomping. Even with the noise from the stomping and the wall of animals, I could still hear my heart beating above it all. A large brown bear pounded into the clearing. Sanj and Dustin both stepped back.

"So there you are, big guy. You took your time," Dustin said.

I quickly looked over at Geeky Girl and tried to mouth a message back to her that said, "Just be careful not to unhypno the bear at the same time, or we're sunk."

Her last mouthed message to me before she pulled the trigger on the ray gun said, "No, don't worry, I won't hit the skunk."

26

The next thing I knew, the wall of forest animals around me started to crumble and fall. Birds flew off to nearby trees or pecked along the ground. Squirrels started digging around in the leaves, raccoons started chasing the squirrels, skunks started waddling off to wherever it is skunks normally go, and groundhogs just kinda sat there looking like grumpy groundhogs, really.

Geeky Girl ran over to me with the ray gun in her hand. "I did it, I did it!" She jumped up and down.

"You did it!" Sanj shouted at her. "You've ruined everything!"

"I think you totally ruined stuff first, Sanj," I started to say, but was interrupted by a very loud

"ROOOOOOOOOAAAAARRRR!"

The bear was
shaking its head and
looking around,
obviously confused.
It looked unhappy
and, worst of all, it
looked kinda hungry.

"You unhypnotized
the bear?!" Dustin
screeched.

"Ummm, sorry
about that," Geeky Girl said.

"Ruuuuunnnnnn!" Sanj shouted, and started to
move. Dustin grabbed his arm and held him firmly.

"Stand very still." Dustin spoke quietly in a
very calm voice. "If you run, the bear will run too."

"Good." Sanj nodded. "I want the bear to run."

"The bear will run AT YOU," Dustin added.

"Go for them!" Sanj shouted, and pointed over
toward Geeky Girl and me. Boris flitted down

onto her shoulder, and Fang crept along the ground till she was next to my foot. She kept her eye on the bear the whole time.

Sanj and Dustin now stood on one side of the clearing, and we were on the other. The bear stood between us. We were like statues: the only movement came from some slightly dazed groundhogs and squirrels still wandering around, bumping into things.

"We have to trap the bear somehow," I said, trying to use a calm voice like Dustin had done, but really feeling my words shaking as they came out.

"Can't you use that whistle thing on it again?" Geeky Girl whispered.

"Not since you've unhypnotized him, I can't," Dustin said.

"Look, I said sorry," Geeky Girl said. "And I've already reprogrammed the ray gun to unhypnotize, so it can't zap him again either."

"The only way that bear is going to give up is when he's already caught and eaten us," Sanj said, "or you ideally."

Then I looked over at Geeky Girl. "Or the bear THINKS he's caught us?"

"Yes!" Geeky Girl very slowly reached into her bag. She gently lifted out the 3-D goggles and started to adjust the controls on the side.

The bear started to sniff the air and scratch the ground.

"This isn't good, people," Dustin said. "He's smelling us and deciding that we would be pretty good to eat."

"What on earth can you do with goggles that will stop the bear? Throw them at him?" Sanj asked. He started backing away and the bear growled again.

I don't know anything, really, about bear behavior, but this bear looked ready to strike. I gently moved my leg in front of Fang to protect her. She rubbed against my ankle, and I felt a little furry shiver travel up my leg. She was scared too. I really hadn't seen Fang scared of many things before. I didn't know what to do.

"OK, it's ready. But how do we get him to wear them?" Geeky Girl asked.

"I'll do it," I said as I took one step forward. Fang pounced on my jacket and clawed her way up to my shoulder. Suddenly, she wasn't shaking anymore. Her grip was strong; I could feel her tail thwack against my jacket.

"**MEEEEEOOOOOOWWW,**"

she kitten-roared, and the bear stared right at her.

27

"Get down, Fang," I whispered. "I'll do this. I don't want you to get hurt."

I scooped her up, and whispered to her, "So just in case the bear wins, which he totally won't, but just in case . . . um . . . thanks, Fang, for saving me from that snake. You totally had my back, and my front, really, and now I gotta do the same for you."

Then I took another small step forward and turned to Geeky Girl. "On three, throw me the goggles, OK?"

She nodded.

"One evil genius, two evil genius, and . . . THREE," I shouted as I tossed Fang to Geeky Girl, just as she tossed me the goggles.

"RRRReEEWWWOOOWWW!" Fang shrieked as she flew through the air.

The bear reared up and growled.

I grabbed the goggles and ran. "AAAARRRR-GGGHHHH!"

"He has totally lost it," Sanj said, covering his eyes.

I ran toward the bear with the goggles in my hand, not really knowing what I was going to do with them. And then, just above the bear, another evil lightbulb appeared, and I suddenly knew what I had to do. I had an evil plan!

I kept on running right past the bear, and just to make sure the bear noticed me, I growled at him as I passed. I really hoped what Dustin said before was true, because I needed that bear to run and to run after me.

"Mark, nooo!" Geeky Girl shouted after me, but I didn't stop.

I could hear a loud growl answering mine, and then big heavy stomps heading behind me. The bear was on my tail.

I could hear Geeky Girl shouting, "Come on, we have to help." And running. And then Sanj saying, "Well, I have to see what happens."

I kept on running, dodging past trees and leaping roots on the ground. I was slowing up, but it wasn't much farther. I could smell hot bear breath on my neck now. I hope you have never smelled hot bear breath, because it is more evil than anything on this camp. Blech.

The growling was in my ear as I jumped over the pile of branches and leaves on the forest floor. "I hope this is the right place!" I called as the bear followed me, and then I heard a crash of leaves and twigs and the thud of a bear hitting the ground. We had hit Bob and Diablo's practice snake pit. I didn't hear any hissing, so either the snake was in the real trap back at camp by now, or it was unlucky and was now snake pancake underneath the bear.

I turned and looked. The bear seemed stunned,

but it was getting up. I had only a second before it would climb out, even madder than before.

I could see that as the bear stood up in the pit, its head was above the line of the ground. I bent down and put the beanie on its head. What I couldn't see was the bear's arm swipe me from the side and knock me forward into the pit. I thwacked onto the ground in front of the bear. This was not part of my mega-evil plan.

The beanie was in place, but I hadn't flipped the switch to turn it on. And until it was turned on, it wasn't a trap, just a bit of bear fashion that wasn't making him any happier.

I heard lots of footsteps above.

"Fang, quick. Bite the switch on the bear hat!!" Geeky Girl shouted.

I heard another "ReEEEEooooowwwwllll!" from Fang as she landed on the bear's head and bit at the hat.

The bear was waving its paws in the air, trying to claw Fang off his head. Then I spotted the budgie dive-bombing him from above.

It looked like a scene in those old movies where King Kong is being attacked by tiny planes. Well, if King Kong was a grumpy bear and the planes were a little green budgie. Boris was distracting him, but it wouldn't last long. I had to get up there and help Fang.

The bear let out a "Rooarrr!" and leaned its head back. Fang nearly fell off, but dug into the bear's thick fur with her paws and held on. Then the bear flung its head forward, and the motion pulled the goggles down over his eyes. Perfect luck! It couldn't see now that his eyes were covered, but the goggles still weren't switched on.

"The button," Geeky Girl shouted just as the bear's paw caught Fang on the side and sent her flying off his head. She tumbled into a pile of leaves and just lay there on the ground. Not moving.

"Fang!" I shouted. Then the bear turned toward my voice and started sniffing in my direction. It couldn't see, but it could still smell me. Right then, though, I didn't care. I was not going to be bear food today, and I was not going to let my kitten be a bear snack.

I wasn't thinking. I clearly wasn't thinking. I mean, what person, who has any kind of thought in their head, jumps on a bear's back? But that's what I did.

The bear reared up again, but I hung on. The bear scrambled out of the pit in a rage. Throwing me right and left, but I hung on. I just had to hit that button. I reached up and whacked the top of those goggles on the bear's head, aiming for the big red button, of course.

"Mark!" Geeky Girl shouted. Then everything went kind of quiet.

I remember falling off the bear. I remember Geeky Girl shouting. I remember Sanj wheezing and hiding behind a bush. I remember being on the ground and seeing a big hairy bear butt heading for me and me rolling out of the way. I think that's when I started thinking again.

I rolled out from under the bear just as his tail hit the grassy floor next to the pit. It stopped swatting, whimpered slightly and covered its ears with its paws. And it just stayed there.

I got up and ran over to Fang, who was still lying in the pile of leaves.

"Fang?"

28

Boris flapped down and started fanning Fang with his wings. I could see a flutter of her eyelids and a twitch of her paw, and then—POUNCE! She was up and just caught the edge of a budgie feather as Boris retreated back to Geeky Girl's shoulder.

"Ah, that's my evil little kitten," I said, stroking her behind the ears.

Sanj strode out from behind the bush. "Well, that's all very touching, but you wouldn't have needed to do any of that if you hadn't messed up our animal trap in the beginning."

Dustin looked at his watch. "It's nearly time to show our traps. Maybe we can quickly fix the ray gun and round up some of the smaller animals to do a demonstration."

"Give us the Nicifying Helpful Minion Ray, Geeky Girl," Sanj demanded. "I'll recalibrate it, and if you're lucky, we won't use it on you."

"Oh, ummm." Geeky Girl smiled. "You can pick it up yourself. I dropped it just over there when the bear got out of the pit and was staggering around."

She pointed over to where the bear was sitting. You could just about see the nozzle of the ray gun sticking out from under his bottom fur.

"It might have a few scratches, but you could just ask him to move." She folded her arms triumphantly and smiled at Sanj.

"Argh!!!!" he shouted.

Dustin walked over toward the bear.

"Right. So if you guys have ruined our trap, then we'll ruin yours." He was going to take the goggles off the bear! "Besides, I reckon I can run fast enough."

"You can't run faster than a bear," Sanj said.

"No, I just have to run faster than you."

Suddenly, Boris swooped down and grabbed the whistle from around Dustin's neck.

"Hey!" he shouted as the whistle chain slid over his head and into the air.

Boris dropped it right into Geeky Girl's hands. "Now what do you think the animals will do when they hear this and they're not under your control. Hmmmm?" She blew the whistle as hard as she could.

Dozens of animals all headed for the noise. They did not seem happy.

A raccoon started for me. He looked a lot scarier than Fang with charcoal on her face. Bigger claws, sharper teeth, more attitude.

"Maybe blowing that whistle wasn't such a great idea?" I said to Geeky Girl.

Then I saw Fang hit the raccoon from the side. It was the best kitten-on-raccoon football tackle in history. It was probably the only one too, but that raccoon was not prepared to come back for more. He ran off into the trees. The other animals were all running around, though, looking confused.

Some of the squirrels had decided that Dustin's hair looked pretty good to hide things in and had jumped on his head and started scrabbling for nuts. "Ah, get them off me! My hair!!!" he shouted, but no one was really listening.

Sanj was too busy swatting at more squirrels and skunks. Now, I know that Sanj is an evil genius and all (he never really let us forget it), but nowhere in that giant evil-computer-genius brain did anything ever tell him maybe it's not a good idea to make a skunk angry. And I would say flailing at one and shouting, "Go away you ignorant, stripy little beast," might make it angry.

The skunk lifted its tail and turned. That was all it took.

In a couple of minutes, we had gone from near death by bear to watching a very smelly Sanj and a squirrel-infested Dustin running back to camp screaming like—well, I was gonna say like girls, but I think Geeky Girl would've hit me, and Dustin couldn't tell on her out here for unauthorized violence at camp, so I didn't.

29

I finished wrapping the last of the clear tape around the bear's head, avoiding his claws as they occasionally swiped at something imaginary in front of him and then went back to covering up his ears. I was making sure those goggles were not gonna fall off.

"It is amazing how many good traps just need a little tape in the end," I said. Geeky Girl nodded.

She and I looked over at the bear as he sat and swatted.

"So," I said as I leaned in to look at the bear, "what image did you program to trap him, anyway?"

"Well," Geeky Girl said, smiling, "we didn't have any bear-appropriate images, really, so I pulled up some old *Star Wars* stuff from my image bank." She paused. "He's basically being held prisoner by Ewoks with little lightsabers."

"And the audio?" I asked, not sure if I wanted to know.

"Oh yeah. The Ewoks are singing," she answered. "It's the best I could do at short notice."

"You are seriously one geeky girl." I laughed. "But you're also pretty evil when you wanna be."

"I guess we should go tell someone about the bear and the goggles and all," she said, then looked at her watch. "But we're going to miss the trap demonstrations. There's no way we can get them all to come down here and see this."

"So we survived the bear, but we're gonna lose anyway and be sent home." I kicked the grass. "Oh man! And I hate canoes too."

Then Fang's ears perked up and Boris fluttered up to Geeky Girl's shoulder again. I heard some more stomping coming up to the clearing.

"You don't think the bear has a friend, do you?" Geeky Girl said nervously as we stared at the edge of the woods. "I hope not, because we only have one set of those goggles."

Fang dropped into total attack-kitten stance. I don't know if she thought she could now take on any bear, but she looked like she was ready to try.

That's when we heard the singing. "Urgggh, urghhh, urghhh, urghh, urghhh urgh . . ."

"Igor!" Geeky Girl and I said at the same time.

Igor stomped out from the trees and motioned back the way he'd come. He mimed a pretty good impression of what must have been Dustin trying to pull squirrels out of his hair, and then just pinched his nose and wheezed for Sanj.

"Yup," I said. "They ran back to camp after we totally took down their trap with like a million hypnotized animals all attacking at once and then"—I paused and stepped back to reveal our captured bear—"we totally trapped a bear."

"URGH!" Igor said, and fist-bumped me.

"I know, right?" I said.

"But that doesn't help us win the contest," Geeky Girl said. "I mean, I'm not all about the winning, but it would be nice to show those leaders and the other campers that we did this. And . . . I sort of don't want to go home yet, even though I didn't want to be here."

Igor then mimed what I guessed must have been him paddling the Canoe of Shame and sinking. I don't think he trusted the canoe would last long with him in it.

They both sighed.

I stepped forward. "Well, I am all about the winning," I said. "I want that Evil Emperor of the Week crown."

"You know they don't actually give you a crown, right?" Geeky Girl said.

Igor mimed holding a certificate.

"I'm getting a crown!!!!" I shouted. "I don't care if I have to make it myself, but I'm winning that prize too." I looked at Geeky Girl and Igor. "We all are. All we have to do is get the bear back to camp," I said.

"Igor, how much do you think you can carry? And how heavy is an average bear?"

30

You should have seen their faces. Kirsty, Trevor and Phillipe were all on the stage by the front of the campfire and the rest of the campers were all gathered around when we walked up.

One Geeky Girl (walking a little taller than she had all week).

One Uber-Tough Bear-Trapping Evil Emperor in the making (you know that's me, right?).

And one Igor, carrying a bear in a beanie with goggles.

Oh yeah, and one small gray stripy charcoal-colored raccoon and one smudgy gray bird. No one noticed them but us, and that's just the way we wanted it.

Bob and Diablo were on the stage in the front

as well. Kirsty was holding a certificate that said "Evil Camp Emperor," and it looked like she was about to hand it to them.

Dustin was sitting off to the side mumbling to himself and scratching his head. It looked like they had to shave off part of his hair. And Sanj was sitting in a barrel of tomato juice to get rid of the skunk smell.

"There is one more trap to judge," I said to the stunned crowd of campers.

Igor walked right up to the center of the stage and sat the bear down on the floor right between Kirsty and Trevor.

"You trapped a bear?" Kirsty said.

"That's our bear!!!" Sanj whined. He shrugged so hard that he spilled about a gallon of juice out the side of his barrel.

"That is kind of true. They trapped the bear first. Then she untrapped it," I said, and pointed to Geeky Girl. "Then we retrapped it, only better." I smiled. "So it's a double-cross trap that is even more evil than a single trap. So take that." I fist-bumped Igor.

The camp leaders all looked around at the bear and the goggles.

"That's pretty impressive, but I'm not sure that it would work on all enemies," Phillipe said.

"That's where you're wrong," Geeky Girl spoke up. "The goggles can be adapted to trap anyone in a virtual prison. They think they are being held prisoner for real, so they don't try to get away."

"Ingenious," Trevor the Tech-in-ator said. "Evil ingenious."

"Well, it wouldn't have to be used for evil—" Geeky Girl started to say, but I jumped in fast.

"Thanks, Trevor. May I call you Trevor?" I said.

"No," he answered.

"Right, Mr. Tech-in-ator, I think this is the most evil trap ever, because you have to have some pretty evil programming skills to use it. And you could disguise it as something else and have someone sitting there trapped and no one would see them."

Phillipe nodded and smiled.

"And its kind of eco-friendly because it's reusable," Geeky Girl added. They all looked blankly at her as I elbowed her. "But, yeah, it's totally evil."

"Urgh!" Igor agreed.

"So did Igor plan this trap with you two as well? We heard that his own trap partnership failed," Phillipe said.

The Goth girl that Igor was paired up with huffed and threw down a big broken net.

"Well, Igor didn't plan it with us exactly . . . ," Geeky Girl started.

"But the plan totally wouldn't have worked without him," I said. "He was our evil-plan executor."

Kirsty leaned over and waved a hand in front of the bear. "It's totally trapped," she said. "This might be the evil trap we've been looking for." She nodded to Phillipe and Trevor.

Bob and Diablo both reached over to see if they could grab the certificate from Kirsty and make a run for it, but she was too fast for them.

"Nice try, boys, but no way that you two win Evil Emperor of the Week now. The bear trap wins!" Kirsty announced.

"Yes!" I fist-pumped the air. In the excitement of the moment, Geeky Girl actually went to hug Igor, but decided on a gentle high five instead.

Everybody "Mwhaaa-haa-haa-haa-ed" and clapped. Even the kid still stuck in the bubble. Well, you could see him doing it, even if you couldn't hear it.

"They can't win. They smuggled their own pets onto camp. There, I said it. Now you have to send them home." Sanj splashed more juice out of his barrel as he slapped his hands down in protest.

"Where are zee pets?" Trevor asked.

"Well, they were there in the woods. We trapped them, and then they got away, but they were there!" Sanj said. "Dustin—back me up. You saw the pets!"

All Dustin could mumble, though, was "Squirrels, squirrels. I really hate squirrels" over and over again. Fair enough, really.

"So who gets sent home in the Canoe of Shame?" Diablo asked.

"Skunk Kid and Squirrel Boy?" Bob added.

"Lucky for them we had already picked the worst team of the week," Kirsty said. "Or they would have been paddling away this afternoon."

"This week, we decided to name the submarine trap as the worst team. Mostly because they definitely failed and were already sailing halfway home," Phillipe said.

"So ve just stuck a 'Shame' sticker on zee side of zee sub and sent zhem off," Trevor added. "It saves us going and picking up zee canoe later."

I could see Sanj sigh and sink back down into his barrel of juice.

Then the three counselors lined up onstage and called Geeky Girl, Igor and me forward as the evil kid with the piccolo played.

I could just about see out of the corner of my eye, Fang (aka the raccoon) and Boris (aka nonspecific random forest bird that's certainly not a budgie) paw and wing-bump as Geeky Girl, Igor and I got our certificates. Result!

31

So that's it. My first week at Evil Scientist Summer Camp was over.

I thought I would make a list.

TOP FIVE THINGS I LEARNED AT EVIL SCIENTIST SUMMER CAMP THIS WEEK

5. Snakes don't like me, and I don't like snakes or real raccoons or skunks, and even the groundhogs looked a bit creepy, actually, and don't get me started on bears. Basically wild animals are out.

4. Sometimes when you pretend something,

it comes back to bite you in the butt.
Sometimes this happens like a metaphor-
type thing. Sometimes this happens for real.

3. Geeky Girl has a better evil laugh than most
of the kids here (but still not better than me).

2. Crowns are always way better than certificates.
Why doesn't anyone else get that?

1. Fang is the evilest, most hard-core, snake-
knotting, bear-jumping, raccoon-fighting,
feet-snuggling vampire kitten any Evil
Scientist could wish for (and she still makes
Bob sneeze, which is a total bonus), but my
fingers are covered in Band-Aids. She's still
kinda bitey.

Dear Mom,

Eco-Scientist camp is good.

I'm having fun, but I'm running out of Band-Aids. Please send more.

Oh, and maybe some Oreo cookies.

And my latest copy of Evil Scientist magazine.

And ya know, maybe a crown, if you have one lying around.

Oh, and you can tell Sami that I actually gave a bear a new hat.

Mwhaaa-haa-haa-haa-haa.

Can't wait until next week.

Your son,
Mark

P.S. Sanj got skunked.

ACKNOWLEDGMENTS

There is a great British phrase that I've picked up living in London: "Having kittens!"

It means getting upset or stressed about something. So, I want to thank everyone in my life who has kept me from "having kittens" while I was writing about them.

First I have to thank my amazing, kitten-loving editor, Holly West, for her patience, planning and humor throughout. Thanks as well to Jean Feiwel and the whole team at Feiwel and Friends, especially Brittany Pearlman, who have been fantastic to work with again.

Thanks to my one-in-a-million agent, Gemma Cooper, who kept me writing, kept me running and kept me sane (mostly), and to our clan of

writers in Team Cooper for coffee, cake and
friendship.

Thanks to SCBWI and CWISL for connecting
me with writers and readers and giving me
brilliant support.

And an epic thank-you to my wonderful family,
who have always made me smile and kept me
grounded. I love you guys.

But mostly, thanks to my kittens, Jinx and Echo,
for being the best bitey, swipey, cuddly inspirations
that any writer could ask for.

GOFISH

MO O'HARA

Did you ever go to summer camp as a kid?
I never did go away to summer camp as a kid. I remember watching movies and seeing kids have these amazing camp adventures and thinking it would be cool, but I never went. I did go to weekend Girl Scout camp once, and raccoons broke into our food containers and ate all our food. I think that's why I have a sneaky raccoon in the book.

Mark "The Snake-in-ator" became known as the camper who got rid of pests. What would your summer camp skill be?
Raccoon Wrangler maybe? I could be the Pied Piper of pesky raccoons.

Can you tell us a little bit about the inspiration for Fang?
Pretty much the inspiration for Fang is my own little vampire kittens. I have two adorable and sweet, but pretty bite-y, kittens.

If you had to take Phillipe's disguise class, what would you camouflage yourself as?
I think I would love to be disguised as a waterfall. I like a challenge. ☺

What is your favorite word?
My new fave word is "pareidolia," which sounds like it could be a disease or a tiny country in Eastern Europe, but it's actually a word for the psychological condition where you see faces in inanimate objects. Like when you think a house looks surprised or a car looks happy or when people see the image of the face of someone famous in a cinnamon bun. I do this all the time (although I have never actually seen a famous person in a bun), but I see expressions and faces in buildings and in things. It's nice to know there's a word for it.

If you could have any pet in the world, what would it be?
I would love to have a woolly mammoth, but I bet they are a pain to clean up after.

When did you realize you wanted to be a writer?
When I was a kid, I desperately wanted to be an actor, a writer, and a marine biologist. Then I discovered that I get seasick in the smallest amount of water possible (I get a bit queasy in the bathtub). So, long boat trips studying sharks had to get crossed off the list. I feel okay, though, because I did grow up to become an actor and a writer at least.

What is your writing process?
My process isn't the same for every series that I write, but generally I write down ideas in a notebook. I carry a notebook with me everywhere and jot things down when I'm on the bus or waiting in the car or when I pick up my kids. I get to the point where I have lots of scenes and dialogue written in the notebook. Then I type out a plan and talk that over with my editor. After that I start writing the first draft. It takes a few drafts to get things right, though.

What is the best advice you have ever received about writing?
Just do it! Sit down and write, even when you are not in the mood. Shake up your writing, too. If you normally write funny stories, try writing something scary. If you normally write romance, try writing something funny instead. You'll learn something new by trying a new style or genre. Give it a go.

What do you want readers to remember about your books?
I want them to remember the characters, the adventures, and of course, the evil laugh. Mwhaaa-haa-haa-haa.

What happens when an aspiring evil scientist
and his mostly evil (and totally forbidden) vampire
kitten blast off to Evil Scientist Space Camp?
Let the Epic Evil Spaceness begin!

Keep reading for an excerpt.

This summer just got a little bit more epic. The camp counselors announced that our next challenge at Evil Scientist Summer Camp will be led by the totally awesome evil astronaut Neil Strongarm!! Yes, I said that right. Neil Strongarm. The Evil Astronaut, not the other guy. He is to astronauts what a triple-dip hot-fudge sundae with extra sprinkles is to plain old ice cream. Epic!

And I will actually get to meet him in real life! I've planned twenty-seven impressive things to say to him, come up with two cool new evil inventions, and even ironed my white evil-scientist coat. (As Neil says on page fifty-three of his autobiography, "You have only one chance to make an evil impression.")

Anyway, for one week Camp Mwhaaa-haa-ha-a-watha is turning into Evil Space Summer Camp. I am ready. Let the epic evil spaceness begin.

—The Great and Powerful Mark

"I just don't get it," Geeky Girl said for the third time.

"He's an astronaut and he's evil." I paused for her to take it in. "So he's an evil astronaut."

Geeky Girl's face looked like she was trying to figure out how to divide a really big number or something. Then she shook her head again. "He can't be both."

"Yes, he can," I said.

"Urgh," agreed Igor. Igor was a kid of few words. OK, no words, but he knew his stuff about evil celebrities.

Geeky Girl kept talking. "But how can a person spend time in the vastness of space and look back at the small, fragile blue marble—"

"Wait, they play marbles in space?" I interrupted.

"But that would be stupid 'cause, like, they wouldn't really roll, just float around—"

"I meant the Earth!" she interrupted back. "Because it looks like a blue marble from far away in space! How could someone look back on the fragile blue marble that is the Earth and not want to do something positive with their lives?"

I slumped down onto the bench. "Igor, show her the book."

The Man Who
Should Have Been
THE FIRST MAN
ON THE MOON

Igor went over to one of the beds in the tent and picked up a hardback biography of Neil Strongarm. He handed it to Geeky Girl. "Urgh, urgh," he said.

She read the title, "*The Man Who Should Have Been the First Man on the Moon*," and then flipped it over to read the blurb on the back. "'One day, as I looked out of the spacecraft window back at the spinning blue marble in the vastness of space, I had a thought about my destiny.' See!" she said smugly, and then kept reading. "'I looked at the Earth, so tiny, and all the stars around it, and I thought, World domination is for wimps! I want it all! Space and everything!' Noooo . . ." Geeky Girl whimpered.

"I told you," I said. "Neil Strongarm is actually evil and he's actually an astronaut and he is actually coming here to camp to run the contest this week. This is gonna be so epic!!"

"Urgh, urgh, urgh," Igor added.

"Reeeooowl!" Fang jumped up on the book and clawed at the picture of Neil Strongarm on the cover.

"Hey, kitten, watch the book jacket." I scooped her up and put her on the bed next to Geeky Girl.

"I don't think Fang likes Neil Strongarm," Geeky Girl said.

"She hasn't even met him yet," I said. "And I can't exactly go up to him and introduce them, can I? Illegal pet in camp? Fang and I would be on the first canoe out of here."

"Urgh, urgh." Igor nodded his head.

BBBRRRRUUUUUUUUUUUUUMMMMMM!

Then the ground started to rumble. "Whhhooooaaaa," I said, grabbing the bench so I didn't fall off.

Fang dug her claws into the mattress and Geeky Girl's jeans to steady herself. "Owwwww, Fang!"

Geeky Girl unhooked Fang's claws from her now partly shredded jean leg. "What is that noise?"

"URGH!!!!" Igor shouted from the tent flap as he peered out. "Urgh, urgh!"

"He's here?!" I jumped off the bench and ran to the tent flap with Igor to look out.

"Who? And how do you know that's what Igor meant?" Geeky Girl said, standing up to join us.

"You spend long enough in a tent with a guy and you learn what his *urgh*s mean," I said. "It's Neil Strongarm's transport shuttle. It just landed."

Then the kid with the trumpet that gives us our evil wake-up call in the mornings started to play. There was a kid on the drums with him this time, though, too.

Dum ... dum ... dum .... DA DUM! the trumpet started. Then the drum kicked in. *Boom, boom boom boom boom boom boom boom boom boom.*

"Is that the movie theme from *2001: A Space Odyssey*?" Geeky Girl said.

"Yeah, he learned a new evil space tune in honor of Neil Strongarm," I said. "I would be worried that it might impress Neil, but really, when you spend time in small echoey spaceships, the last thing you want to hear is a lot of loud music."

Igor nodded again.

"So, did you come up with any plans to impress Neil Strongarm yet?" I asked Geeky Girl.

"I don't even think I want to impress an evil astronaut," she said, and shrugged.

"'Cause I've come up with some of my best evil inventions yet. I'm going to offer them to Neil, so he knows that I'm not just any old evil scientist kid. I'm an evil inventor too."

"So what have you got to show him that's so impressive?" she said, crossing her arms.

"OK, first, my Evil Super Space-Expanding Foam—*useful in all space station and spaceship scenarios. Everything from battle repairs to home improvements in space can be made easier with Evil Super Space-Expanding Foam,*" I said in my best TV-commercial voice.

Igor clapped.

"Thanks, dude," I said. "Oh, and Igor and I both came up with the idea for the Pogo Stick Lunar Travel Individual Vehicle. *Useful for low-gravity environments. Cover more ground than walking-jumping. Use less energy. And have way more fun.*"

"A moon pogo stick?" Geeky Girl said. "Yeah, you guys are definitely going to impress him with that."

"Well, *you* haven't done anything," I said. "Look, I know that you didn't want to be stuck in an evil scientist summer camp, not actually being evil an' all, but if you're here, you really gotta make more of an effort." I paused. "Besides, I really like the moon pogo stick thing."

"I told you, I don't care about impressing this guy. You two go for the whole Evil-Emperor-of-the-Week thing with whatever pretend space games he comes up with. I'm not interested," she said.

Geeky Girl pulled back the tent flap and looked at the shuttle as it opened its hatch.

"Hey, do you think he'll show us the plans for his new evil space station, SSSH?" I asked Igor.

"Why do I have to *shhh*?" GG asked.

"You don't," I said.

"You just *shhh*ed me," she said.

"No, his space station that he's building. It's called SSSH—Secret Space Station Homebase. SSSH. Get it?" I said.

"*Sssh*-Urgh," Igor said.

"I get it," she said. "I just don't see what the big deal is about an evil astronaut." Geeky Girl shrugged her shoulders and strolled toward the landing site where all the campers had already started to gather.

Igor and I looked at each other, and then burst into a spontaneous high five. "Because it's the biggest deal ever!" I shouted.

For some FIN-TASTICALLY FISHY mayhem, check out another series by Mo O'Hara:

THE SEAQUEL
MO O'HARA

FINS OF FURY
MO O'HARA

ANY FIN IS POSSIBLE
MO O'HARA

LIVE AND LET SWIM
MO O'HARA

JURASSIC CARP
MO O'HARA

MO O'HARA

ZOMBIEGOLDFISHBOOKS.COM